TACTICAL RESPONSE TEAM ⬟ BOOK TWO

PROTECTOR

CINDY BONDS

Scrivenings
PRESS
Quench your thirst for story.
www.ScriveningsPress.com

Published by Scrivenings Press LLC
15 Lucky Lane
Morrilton, Arkansas 72110
https://ScriveningsPress.com

Printed in the United States of America

Paperback ISBN 978-1-64917-214-3

eBook ISBN 978-1-64917-215-0

All scriptures are taken from the KING JAMES VERSION (KJV): KING JAMES VERSION, public domain.

Editors: Elena Hill and Linda Fulkerson

Cover by Linda Fulkerson, bookmarketinggraphics.com

"But those who hope in the Lord will renew their strength. They will soar on wings like eagles; they will run and not grow weary, they will walk and not be faint." Isaiah 40:31

PROLOGUE

"R un," Danica whispered.

She gripped her sister's hand and pulled, running to the property's edge. Jumping over the weathered fence, Danica landed on the other side, dirt flying up in her face. She scrambled to stand as her younger sister's long legs perfectly rolled and stood her up.

"Did he see us?" Kyra gulped.

"Stop!" the gritty voice boomed in the evening air.

Danica guided Kyra silently, pushing deeper and deeper into the darkness of the woods.

"Dani, you said we wouldn't get caught," Kyra moaned.

"Quiet," Danica hissed. "I didn't think anyone lived there."

They jumped over leaf piles and fallen logs. A strong odor surged as Danica staggered to a halt.

"What's that?"

Danica turned to Kyra's wrinkled nose, glancing behind to see the still forest. "I'm not sure. Probably a dead deer or something. Stay close."

"Dani," Kyra whimpered.

Ignoring her sister, Danica slid between the rocks and brush. The smell grew stronger and stronger. An enormous pile of dirt loomed in a clearing. Danica took one look at the purple shoes pointed to the sky and swallowed the bile in her throat. "This ... this way, hurry!"

Dragging Kyra to the left, Danica raced faster and faster. They had to reach the field, they had to make the clearing. Her heart pounded in her chest.

It can't be her. Danica took a deep breath. *Who else has those purple shoes? And that smell ...*

The trees thinned. Crisp, yellow leaves materialized through the spaces. The tall corn husks reached the sky.

Kneeling where the trees ended, Danica glanced back. "When I say run, sprint to the house and don't stop. Promise me." Danica stared into her twelve-year-old sister's teary eyes. "Promise you won't stop for anything."

"I ... I promise," Kyra sobbed.

At the rustle and crash of leaves, Danica stood, yanking once more on Kyra's arm. "Run!"

Racing through the dried corn husks, Danica viewed Kyra's disappearing form.

God, don't let her get caught because of me.

Only one thing made that smell, only one person had those shoes on all the time, but Tony had mentioned she was on vacation with his little sister ...

A gunshot sounded. Danica screamed as heat seared through her shoulder. Her heart pounded, and she closed her eyes.

1

Fourteen Years Later

S moke and debris covered the windows as Haiden Blake let out a billowy breath.

"I've got no shot," he mumbled into the com.

Swinging the rifle to the left, he traced the movements of the rest of his team. Jeff Powers directed as Evan Mitchell and Sergio Chavez followed.

His jaw clenched.

Where is she?

Lifting from the scope, he peered into the crisp winter morning. Frost in the air, stillness settled across the overgrown yard. The empty business complex before him had several entrances—too many for their small team to cover. They were supposed to be backup.

But a gunshot had them advancing without a police presence.

"We're entering the side door. You see anything?"

Haiden gritted his teeth at Jeff's voice. Still no sign of her. Foggy windows obscured his view. No movement, no sign of a shooter. "Nothing. No visual."

"Check."

Jeff entered first, Sergio holding the door. Haiden fixed his gaze on his team through hazy first-floor windows. The trio began a slow walk down the hallway. Haiden tracked them.

Raising the scope to the next floor, a wisp of movement directly above the team made him pause. "Possible sight. Hold."

Whatever was still clouding the windows made it impossible to see clearly.

"Movement above, nothing now. Finding a clear line of sight."

"Go." Buck Thompson's gravelly voice sounded.

Shifting up, Haiden snatched his rifle and headed to the left. Perhaps the other side of the building would give him a better view.

Still no sign of her. She'd better be somewhere safe.

"Stop!" Jeff's voice echoed through the com.

Jumping a log, Haiden's heart pounded as gunshots echoed from the building.

"Engaged, taking fire."

With a groan, Haiden dropped to the ground and set up once more. Black vests and quick motion led his sight to the left. There, a man leaned over the stairs, a rifle in his hands.

"Got sight. Above you on the stairwell."

"Yeah, we know," Evan gritted.

More shots fired.

"Haiden? You able to get a shot?" Buck asked.

"Not clear," Haiden responded.

As the shooter stood, Haiden took a breath, letting out a smooth exhale as his finger rested on the trigger.

"DON'T MOVE." Danica Freeman aimed her rifle at the man in the stairwell.

"Why not?" His sneer echoed in the empty building.

"You've got a bead on you right now. Our sniper will shoot if you don't drop your weapon and raise your hands."

"Nice try."

Danica sighed. "Do it."

A shot shattered the window, the bullet embedding into the wall behind the man. He screamed, reaching for his shoulder as he turned.

"Drop it! Now!" Danica lowered as he spun to her, lining up her shot.

Another piercing bullet fired, and the man fell backward, his rifle dropping as he hit the floor.

"Dani?" Jeff came flying up the stairs from behind the body.

"I'm good." She stood as Jeff cleared the man. "Did you fire?"

Jeff shook his head, Evan and Sergio coming in behind him. "Not us."

Gripping her weapon, she motioned behind her. "Let's clear it."

In ten minutes, they had the two-story building cleared. They found two women locked in a closet, wrists and ankles bound. A kidnapping gone wrong? Thankfully, the Tactical Response Team arrived before the captors had time to move them, or worse.

"All good?"

Danica turned her gaze from the women sitting with the police and nodded at Buck as he approached. "What happened? How did we beat the police here?"

"We were detained. Glad you guys were here to handle it." An officer stepped around Buck with an extended hand. "Sergeant Sutton."

She shook his hand with a nod. "Detained?"

"It was unexpected. Won't happen again." Sutton grinned. "But it looks like you didn't need our help."

"We're always here for back up," Buck gritted out. "But back up only. Next time, get a call to me or to Jeff Powers. This is your show, not ours."

"I appreciate the concern."

"Sir?" A uniformed officer approached.

Sutton gave a wave. "I've got to go talk to these young ladies. Thanks again." He walked off with the officer in tow.

"That could've ended badly if we hadn't been here," Danica muttered.

Buck stood, staring after Sutton.

"Buck?"

"Yeah?"

"Are you okay?"

He nodded. "What could possibly detain the police when an eyewitness called in a woman running, followed by shots fired?"

"So, there were three?" Danica shivered at the cold breeze and the thought of that man kidnapping three girls.

"The police are sweeping the area. They're having trouble IDing the caller. I'm sure they'll find her."

Jeff approached. "Did he give a reason for the police showing late?"

"Detained."

Jeff frowned at her explanation. "That isn't an excuse."

A group of officers rushed past, carrying a woman wrapped in a blanket.

"She was in a culvert. Get her to the ambulance!"

Danica blew out a breath, relieved at the third woman being found.

"Let's get back to the office and recap." Buck nodded to the group and turned toward his vehicle.

As Danica gathered her things, a deep drawl came from behind her.

"You good?"

Turning with a flinch, Haiden stood a few feet away, but she never sensed his approach.

"Of course. And I had him." She narrowed her eyes. "You didn't have to take that shot."

"He was turning with a gun," he mumbled.

"I had it covered."

Haiden nodded, his jaw clenched as he searched the area. "Where were you?"

"What do you mean?"

"I had no line of sight, but when I did, you weren't there." His green eyes stared into hers.

"I went around back to see if I could find another entrance."

He grunted and stepped closer. "Bad move, Dani. No back-backup," he took a breath. "You can't just go in without backup."

"Buck was following me in. He went left, I went right."

"We had no information other than a shooter. What if someone had rigged the building? What if there had been more than one shooter?"

Working her jaw back and forth, she ended the conversation before she let Haiden have a piece of her mind. "Let's just drop it, okay?"

"Dani."

She stepped forward. "I can handle myself. Thanks for the concern." Spinning, she struggled against tears as she neared the SUV.

Sliding the gear into the back, her heart hurt.

Slamming the SUV door, she started up the car and gripped the steering wheel. The last three months had been a miserable, uncomfortable silence between her and Haiden, and she was ready for it to end. She longed for normal again.

What now, God?

2

J eff followed Buck to the SUV and slid into the passenger
seat.

"How's things with Danica?"

Jeff let out a huff. "Like she would tell me. What do you want
to know?"

Buck frowned.

"Look, this Haiden thing, I'm not sure what's going on, but I
thought it was all better after the gala. They're at least talking
now."

"I'm trusting you to handle that for me. If I need to make a
change, or if they stop working well together—"

"I don't think either of them will let it get that far." Jeff
chewed on the inside of his cheek. "I am, however, concerned
about the police being detained."

"Don't let it get to you. I'll handle it."

"Handle what? What do you know?"

Buck shrugged. "Nothing, yet. But I am going to make sure it
doesn't happen again."

Jeff nodded as he stared out the window. "I've not met Sutton
before. You?"

"Nope. Must be a transfer."

"The fact he didn't give a reason for them being late, that's odd."

"Like I said, I'll handle it."

Jeff snickered. Buck was retired military, a Ranger. He wanted things run by the book. Being 'detained' wasn't something that happened or was acceptable. Poor Sutton had no idea what was coming.

The ambulance pulled out in front of them, and Jeff's jaw clenched.

Those three women had depended on the police to save them. Maybe Sutton deserved whatever Buck was ready to dish out.

"YOU'RE WORKING WITH US? OFFICIALLY?" Danica jumped from her chair and squeezed Bexley tightly. "I'm so excited!"

"Oh, good grief, Danica. You're acting like you're surprised." Evan smirked, a wonderful reprieve from his usual frown.

"I *am* surprised. It's not like Buck discusses these things with me. Jeff, maybe, but not me." Danica worked to ease the nervousness in her voice.

"Well, for right now, I'll be in charge of media relations while I get back into training."

"That's great." Sergio pulled Bexley to him and gave her a hug too.

Danica nearly burst into laughter as Evan's face went red. Leave it to him to get jealous of the one man in the group who was married.

"Glad you're official." Haiden nodded.

"Well, I've been invited to start training. Not sure official is the word. I've got a lot to do before I'm up and running at the pace this group carries."

"You'll do fine." Jeff entered and gave her a nod. "I think

those skills you learned as a special operations agent will be useful."

"You mean if we ever have another person to put into protection?"

Evan huffed and gave Bexley a wink. "That was a onetime thing."

"I'm flattered." Bexley sat back down at the island with Evan.

Danica stood, opening the fridge. "I'm hungry. What's for lunch?"

"It's barely nine in the morning. You not eat breakfast?"

Frowning at Haiden's voice from behind her, she shrugged. "I had a granola bar. It was too early for a big meal." As she turned, she maneuvered around his body and to the walk-in pantry. Peering at the boxes of cereal, she sighed. "What?"

Haiden leaned against the doorway, his arms crossed. "You gonna tell me why you're upset?"

"Who says I'm upset?"

"I'm not stupid."

"I would never say you were."

"Then talk."

He was so much like Buck, it was infuriating. All her life, her uncle Buck had treated her like the daughter he didn't have. Which worked, since he was the dad she needed. She was raised with one-word answers or phrases, quick clips of conversation where there wasn't much to fill in.

"I can handle myself. But lately, you just jump in, take over like you think I can't cut it."

"I'm doing my job."

"Your job is taking over?"

"My job ... is to protect. I oversee. I see what is about to happen before it does." He leaned forward into her space. "I would never say you can't cut it. I-I know you can."

"So, let me do my job."

His jaw jumped as he turned and walked off.

"Nice conversation?"

Rolling her eyes at Bexley, Danica pushed past and grabbed her purse from the table. "I'm going to get something to eat," she mumbled.

Walking out to the car, she turned at the sound of footsteps behind her.

Bexley made her way to the passenger side door. "Open it up, let's go."

Letting out a sigh, Danica pushed the button to unlock the car and slid in behind the wheel.

"Where're we going?"

She started the car and backed out of the drive. "I don't know. Just somewhere else."

"Coffee?"

She nodded and headed toward their favorite café.

"Why're you mad at Haiden?"

"He interferes."

"With what?"

Danica cut her eyes at Bexley. "My job. I don't see him taking shots for the guys. Last week, he almost pushed me down when we were trying to stop that car from escaping."

"So, he saved you from getting hit by a car?"

"Bex."

"Look, I'm not sure what's going on, but it's not him interfering. You're upset because he blew you off." Bex held up her hands in a hear-me-out gesture. "And you have a right to be."

Danica continued the drive in silence. Once parked outside the café, she slid from the seat and followed Bexley inside. They placed an order, then maneuvered to a back booth.

"Tell me what's really bothering you. I know there's something other than him blowing you off. You wouldn't let that interfere with your work."

Danica leaned against the booth's backrest, gripping her mug with both hands. "I've been grasping lately. Trying to find my footing. After the bombing last fall and almost losing you and Haiden, things have been off."

"You didn't lose us." Bexley winked as she took a sip.

"I know, but it was a very trying situation. I'm not used to, I guess I just ..."

"You feel like maybe you owe Haiden for protecting you."

Danica sat forward. "Haiden shielded my body with his, so I didn't get covered in glass. He was off duty for two weeks, and he had to have surgery."

"He did what anyone one of us would do. You just feel like you owe him."

Danica stared at her friend, and her face heated. It was true.

"Then that whole ignoring you thing—that wasn't cool." Bexley made a face. "I should've knocked some sense into him. Or asked Evan to do it."

Danica chuckled. "I guess I haven't been very understanding. And the whole ignoring me thing, I think it embarrassed him once he found out I stayed with him until he woke up. That's when he just ... stopped talking to me."

Sipping her coffee, Danica's thoughts went to Haiden. His back already held scars. Although she did not know what they were, the doctor had been interested in where they came from.

Now, after shielding her, he had even more scars.

"He's been trying to talk to me lately. I guess I should talk to him."

"You mentioned getting in more time at the range. That would be something you could do."

Danica frowned. "You're not trying to fix something up, are you?"

Bexley shrugged. "Just trying to help you deal with whatever's bugging you. You've got something else going on besides Haiden?"

Going into the chaos of her past wasn't something she wanted to explain.

"Dani?"

"I'm good." She smiled and sat back in the booth. "How about you and Evan?"

Bexley grinned.. "Good, very good. I think he's got something planned for Valentine's Day."

"That's like, two weeks away."

Bexley shrugged.

"Humph," she mumbled. "I could've done without that."

Bexley laughed out loud. "Well, if you have a good conversation with Haiden, maybe you could have something planned for Valentine's Day too."

"You know that never works out—work relationships."

"I don't know, Dani ..."

It would be great, but chances of a relationship with Haiden dropped after the gala. Maybe God would present someone else, someone who might actually understand what she was going through and the pains of her past.

Her phone dinged.

Hey, Dani. Wanted to see what's going on.

Frowning at the text from Tony Carlyle, she let out a sigh.

Nothing much. How're you?

"Is that a friend?"

She cut her eyes to Bexley. "Old friend."

Shuddering at the memories, she pocketed the phone.

3

Haiden slammed down the last round of weights with a grunt.

"Pushing hard, man."

Ignoring Evan, Haiden grabbed his towel and water bottle.

"You got plans for Valentine's?"

Stopping mid sip, Haiden glared up at a grinning Evan. "What?"

Evan shrugged. "Just trying to get your attention. You've been more than unusually quiet today."

"Not quiet, just thinking."

"Like I said, plans?"

Shaking his head, Haiden stood. "Nope."

"You should."

Tossing the water bottle on the table, he turned. "Why?"

"That's what I'd like to know. Why don't you want to make plans with Danica? She's friendly, easy to talk to, and pretty. Don't think I didn't notice when I started. So, why not?"

Shaking his head, Haiden adjusted the weights on the bar, then lay down on the bench. After pushing out reps, Evan helped him place the bar back on the rack.

Haiden sat up and took a deep breath. "I'm guessing you have plans?"

Evan grinned. "Sure do. Going to be a great Valentine's Day."

Haiden huffed and stood from the bench, stretching out his shoulders and ignoring the pull of the recent scars as they strained.

"Your back good?"

Haiden nodded. "Just pulls sometimes."

Evan snatched up the dumbbells and started on curls. "About that. We never talked about your visitor at the hospital."

Haiden glared. "Nothing to talk about."

As Evan dropped the dumbbells in place, he stepped back and put his hands on his hips, his breaths heavy. "Just thought I'd offer. It stays between us if you want to."

Shaking his head, Haiden set the bench for the leg press.

His dad.

Danica had been there when Haiden woke. The feeling of her up against him, holding him and hugging him as he waited for the doctor to examine his injured back. Her face against his bare chest, her hands gripping his side—it had unnerved him much more than he wanted to admit. Then his father showed up, suddenly, unexpectedly, and unwelcomed.

Haiden let the weight drop as he bent his knees, taking a few deep breaths.

The one time he'd taken off his shirt last year in the weight room, Evan spotted the scarring across his back. All Haiden said was 'my dad,' and apparently, Evan hadn't forgotten.

It was an act of God that allowed Haiden into the Army. He didn't meet the medical standards, but the recruiter took the paperwork and said, "You've got a future with us. I hear you can shoot." It was a chance at life and proved God was guiding him through the fire, giving him a future.

"Earth to Haiden."

Haiden cut his eyes to Evan and slid off the bench. "Yeah?"

"Buck wants everyone in the living room ASAP."

He nodded to Evan and wiped his face and neck down with the towel. "Give me a sec."

Evan left out the door as Haiden leaned his palms to the wall. Letting out a deep breath, he rotated his upper body downward, stretching out his shoulders.

"A future. I have a future and t-that's enough," he whispered.

DANICA'S FACE flushed when Haiden made his way from the weight room to the living room. He pulled a chair from the dining room table and sat behind the couch.

His arms and shoulders bulged from the workout, and she forced her eyes away. Bexley bumped her arm.

"Sure you don't want to have a conversation?" Bexley whispered.

"Shut-up," she mumbled.

Ignoring Bexley's chuckle, Danica leaned back against the couch, propping her head up on the arm. Attraction was one of those things she couldn't just drop. He had some major walls built up, and that should be enough to make her want to ignore all lingering feelings.

But it would not make the attraction disappear. At least it wouldn't for her.

"I had a talk with Captain DeSalis. He informed me that the officers being detained today wouldn't happen again. However, even if it does, we have to be prepared like we were for whatever the scene holds."

"That's it? No actual explanation for what happened?" Jeff leaned forward on his knees.

"If he's got internal issues, I trust he'll figure it out. It's not my business. So, starting tomorrow, we'll be going through tactical training and hitting the range. Hard. We've got a new member training with us, and we need to place her into position so everyone can adjust."

"Thanks, Bex," Danica muttered, and Bexley elbowed her again.

"Get your rest in today. You'll need it for tomorrow."

As Buck left, Danica closed her eyes and leaned her head back. Between Bexley's revelation about her owing Haiden and seeing him like that, she was in trouble.

Why in the world was she still so hung up on Haiden Blake?

4

J eff came downstairs early to see Danica preparing a big breakfast.

"Hungry?" He grinned.

"I just figured after Buck's little speech yesterday, I'd need my energy."

"That's a great idea."

His phone buzzed.

Got plans today?

"Weird."

"What?"

"This is the third or fourth text I've received from Tony in the last couple of weeks."

"Why is that weird?" Danica leaned against the island, munching on a piece of bacon.

He shrugged. "I mean, we've always kept in touch, but never really hung out. Between his shifts at the hospital and my work here, it's one of those hit-or-miss things. You talked to him lately?"

"Actually, he texted yesterday out of the blue. Just asking what was going on, but I never heard back from him."

Jeff sat at the island and texted back.

We're training today, so yeah, lots of plans! You wanna meet for lunch this week?

Glancing up, Jeff set his phone down on the island. "Hey, Buck asked me the other day if you and Haiden were okay."

Danica's face went red. "Why wouldn't we be?"

"Don't do that. It doesn't take a master's in psych, which I have, by the way, to sense that tension."

Danica shrugged. "Just stuff."

"He was a jerk at the gala. You can say that." Jeff snatched his own piece of bacon. "I just wanted to clue you in. If Buck sees it—"

"Don't act like Buck doesn't see things like relationships. Just because he's a bachelor doesn't mean he doesn't notice interactions. You better remember that."

He stood, heading for the coffee pot. "You don't have to worry about me. Relationships are off base for a while."

Danica leaned against the counter next to him as he grabbed the creamer.

"It's been a really long time since Meline. Don't do that," Danica mumbled. "Use that psych degree on yourself and see that punishing yourself for something you can't control isn't a healthy thing."

Clinching his jaw at her ability to see things way too clearly, he took his cup back to the island to sit. "So, I can tell Buck things are good?"

"What things?" Haiden stepped into the kitchen and over to the coffeepot. "Something wrong?"

"Not a thing." Danica glared and Jeff chuckled.

"Nope, everything's good." Raising a cup to the duo, Jeff stood and loaded up a plate, then headed to the table.

He sipped his coffee and watched Haiden tracking Danica's movements in the kitchen as she finished cleaning up. Even though he considered Haiden a friend, Danica was like a sister to him. After Haiden blew her off at the gala, Jeff wanted to give Haiden a piece of his mind.

Setting down his mug, he frowned at the contents of his plate. He loved bacon and eggs, but all the talk of the past had his stomach churning. Forcing a forkful in his mouth, he went through the motions and ate, knowing just as Danica mentioned, he'd need the energy for the day.

AFTER BREAKFAST, Bexley and Evan started cleaning the kitchen while Danica and Haiden finished eating.

"Where's Serg? The funny man is never late for breakfast." She smiled as Evan let out a chuckle and responded.

"He took off this week for his daughter's *quinceañera*."

"Wow, fifteen. Can't believe he has a daughter who's fifteen," she muttered into her plate.

Buck walked through, gear on his back. "Everyone get loaded up. We've got a lot of work to do."

She stood and took her plate to the sink amidst the groanings of everyone. Haiden stood next to her, loading his dishes with a grin on his face.

"Stop being so smug."

His bright green eyes met hers.

"I think I'm going to challenge you today, Haiden."

"That should be fun."

"Oh no, nothing long range. You'd have an unfair advantage."

He shrugged. "We can do short range drills too."

He gave her a wink and her face heated. Pushing away from the counter and Haiden, she hurried upstairs to gather her things.

5

Haiden stifled a chuckle as a red-faced Danica headed up the stairs toward the equipment room.

As he gathered his things, her smile burned into his brain. Danica was an amazing woman. About five inches shorter than him, she had big brown eyes, dark hair that framed her face, and that smile. After seeing her all dressed up at the gala last year, it had taken great restraint to keep his hands to himself and leave with their friendship intact.

Sliding his rifle and equipment into the back of the SUV, he got into the passenger seat next to Evan.

"You're not riding with Danica?"

Haiden glared up at Evan for a moment. "No, why?"

"Just wondering." Evan let a smirk out and he frowned.

"Nothing's going on, Ev. Drop it."

"Oh, I can tell nothing's going on. We *all* can tell nothing's going on."

"Just because you and Bex are together, doesn't mean everyone else needs to couple up." He clenched his jaw and forced the words out, working hard to keep his stutter at bay.

"Yeah, yeah," Evan muttered as he started the SUV and backed out.

Danica came out of the office and paused in the garage for just a moment before heading to her car with her equipment.

Haiden just wanted things to go back to normal, the way they were before the gala when they were friends and the awkward tension didn't exist.

Evan's phone rang, and he took it off Bluetooth.

"Hey."

He and Evan had clicked since they first met. No need to discuss or go into detail with anything. They were two men, comfortable with silence. But now, being around Bexley had forced Evan into a more talkative mood. Just like earlier in the gym.

"Yeah, we're just now headed out." Evan's chuckle sounded. "I'll meet you there ... Love you too. Bye."

Haiden hoped the silence would last until the range, but of course, Evan had other plans.

"Look, man, you know I'm the last person to talk to you about women—"

"Then don't." He glared, but Evan just shook his head.

"I need to tell you, when it's the right person, it's better. Everything is better."

Haiden stared out the window in silence, watching as the scenery whipped by. It's not that he didn't like Danica—there was a reason he didn't want a relationship. A lot of reasons. And he wasn't obligated to explain them to anyone.

Two HOURS LATER, Danica leaned against the box at the range, waiting on Haiden to finish his final run through the training course.

Jeff's eyebrow raised as he walked past toward the exit. She made a face and turned to find Haiden standing behind her.

"Problem?"

"You're way too sneaky."

"In the Army, we call it stealth."

She nodded. "Stealth. I'll remember that."

"You gonna challenge me?"

"Actually, I thought you might give me some pointers."

Haiden's smile spread across his face. Her heartbeat quickened.

"You want pointers? From me?"

"Yes."

"So, I'm not interfering?"

Crossing her arms, she leaned against the box. "I'm asking for help here—don't make it a big deal."

He shrugged. "I'm good with it being a big deal." He sat down his equipment, pushing into her space. "What do you need help with?"

"I pull to the right." She lay out her targets. "I'm to the right of the bullseye each time."

"You're either jerking the trigger or lowering your shoulder. Let me see."

Taking her place in the slot, she put on the earmuffs and slid the chamber of her 9MM. Haiden stood behind her, hands on her shoulders.

"Take aim and squeeze the trigger like you would in close range."

Taking a deep breath, she lined up her shot. Taking two shots, she frowned at the intact bullseye.

"Yeah, lowering your shoulder. Your grip is good. Try again, but this time, keep your aim to the left of the bullseye."

"I don't want to compensate. I want to do it right." Her skin pricked at his chuckle. His face was way too close to her neck. "What's so funny?"

"Nothing. I appreciate you wanting to do it the right way."

She allowed him to shift her stance. "I know how to shoot and how to stand."

"Yes, you do. But if we alter your stance, it might help keep you from lowering your shoulder."

His hands back on her shoulders, he leaned his body in. She took aim once more.

"I'm not going to over-compensate."

"You won't have to." His whispered words in her ear sent a chill down her neck and back that she couldn't stop. "You okay?"

"Perfect," she muttered.

Please, oh please, don't do that again.

Taking a deep breath, she focused on the target.

"Keep your weight even. Shoot when ready." His hands squeezed her shoulders.

After two shots, she pulled off her earmuffs and grinned. "I think I got it."

She put the safety on as Haiden pushed past her and headed down range.

"You got it. Both shots." With a grin, he handed her the target.

She smiled at the missing center. "I think my second shot went a little off."

"That was the first one. You corrected on the second shot. You just need to keep that weight even, and it'll help your shoulders."

"Thanks, Haiden."

He chuckled and patted her back. "Anytime."

"You going to shoot?"

He grabbed up his gear. "Long range. See ya later."

She nodded as he headed to the far end of the range.

Haiden Blake was an amazing man and had a way about him she couldn't understand. With heat bouncing between them, surely, he felt it too. It was as if he pushed for it.

So, why did he walk away every single time?

6

"I just want to know what really happened."

Jeff shook his head as he unlocked the door. Phone to his ear, he tossed his gear inside one-handed. "We gave that report when it happened. Look it up. Nothing's changed in the past three months."

"So, you're saying your team has followed all protocols and hasn't superseded jurisdiction on any of your activities?"

"What?" He slammed the door behind him. "I don't know where that came from, but no. We don't supersede anyone's jurisdiction, and we only arrive on scene when called out by the police. Unless the police call us, we don't show."

"How about yesterday?"

"What about yesterday?"

"Avoiding the question won't help."

Jeff gritted his teeth together. "There is no question. You want to know about yesterday? Talk to the police."

He hung up and shoved the phone in his pocket before grabbing the rest of the gear. Stepping into the equipment room, he stowed his rifle.

"What's up?"

He turned to Danica. "I just had a weird phone call."

"Tony?"

He chuckled as Dani put her gear in the locker. "No, some reporter from the Downtown Dallas News. He insinuated we step outside our authority and don't follow protocol."

She turned with a frown. "What? Where did that come from?"

"No idea. I informed him we only show up when called in by the police, so it's impossible to step outside our jurisdiction. Then I hung up."

"You might need to play things a little nicer. We can't deal with bad PR."

"We've got bad PR?" Bexley walked in carrying her rifle.

Evan followed with the rest of the gear. "What's going on?"

"Jeff got a phone call from a reporter. Something about us over-stepping?" Danica made a face as Bexley sat down.

"Who says we're over-stepping?" Evan slammed the locker shut.

"The reporter didn't reveal his source." Jeff headed out the door and into the kitchen for a water bottle. Bexley and Evan followed. "All I know is that once Buck hears about this, he'll be on the phone trying to track it all down."

"That's a good thing. If Buck can find out who it is, we'll be able to fix it before the situation gets bigger. This kind of stuff always causes problems." Bexley sat on the couch, pushing her legs on the ottoman.

"You've dealt with this?" Jeff asked.

Bexley shrugged. "Not often, but I've been on protection details even after the police or the Feds are called in. They didn't like that our clients wanted to use us instead of their people, and we didn't like that those guys thought they could boss us around. It all leads to bad feelings."

"We work with the same officers on every callout. I play basketball with some of those guys. They would tell me if something was up."

"Give them a call."

Jeff frowned at Evan. "I have a hard time believing it's to that point."

"Don't risk it. Call them now, figure out what's up." Evan sat next to Bexley.

"Yeah, maybe you're right." Jeff turned his phone over on his knee.

What didn't make sense was the reporter calling. He had several friends on the force who would've warned him before a reporter got involved. He stood and headed back down the hallway to his room.

"Hey, where're you going?"

Jeff ignored Danica as he passed the equipment room. "I've got to make a call."

DANICA STOOD at the door watching Jeff, and Haiden smiled. Turning his focus back to his gear, he let out a breath and placed the rifle and his backpack in his locker.

Helping Danica almost did him in. He was a well-trained sniper, but after being so close to her, he barely hit within the target's sixth circle. Even now, his body still buzzed from being so close.

"What's wrong?"

Glancing up, her big brown eyes gleamed. "Just thinking. What's got Jeff so worked up?"

"Some reporter called asking why we overstep our authority and protocols." She leaned against the doorframe, rubbing her left shoulder. "After last year, I know he's been tasked with keeping things calm and fielding a lot of questions."

"I didn't see anyone upset yesterday."

She shrugged. "Neither did I."

He noticed her chewing on the inside of her cheek and grinned. If helping her every day like that ruined his shot, it wouldn't matter to him one bit.

Her phone rang, and she pushed it to her ear.

"Hello?" Her smile widened as she sat down on the bench. "You got an interview? That's awesome! When do you go?"

His jaw clenched. He took his time straightening his things, wondering who she was talking to that made her smile like that.

"Great. Let me know how it goes. Bye."

"Good news?" He glanced over as she stood.

"Yeah, my sister just got a job interview. That's great news."

He smiled as she left the room, still beaming.

Danica was one of those women who stood silently on the sidelines, not asking to be noticed or asking for attention. But she outshined all the others.

Letting out a breath, he sat on the bench with a huff. It was all the talk of relationships, Valentine's Day, today's shooting—he was pulled to her. True, he'd had that pull since the day he met her, but now it was only growing stronger.

"Get a grip," he mumbled as he stood.

This job was important, her friendship was important, and he wasn't willing to risk either for a chance at something more. No matter how much his chest ached and his brain protested. It wasn't worth the risk.

7

By three, the team walked back into the training center. Buck was pacing the room.

"Buck? What's up?" Jeff tossed his gear on the floor.

"It seems we're being targeted."

"Who and why?" Danica sat down, holding her gear in her lap.

"There's a mayoral candidate who has some bad feelings about what happened last year and feels we take unnecessary chances and pose a risk to the city. Apparently, he's taken his concerns to the media instead of simply talking to us."

"What?" Jeff straightened. "This group was formed because the commissioner and the current mayor said they needed more help but couldn't fund it through the state."

"I know," Buck said. "But right now, we're on thin ice. This guy wins, we'll be in trouble."

"Who is he?" Evan's deep voice rumbled through the large room.

"Last name is Roltz."

"That sounds familiar," Danica tapped her chin.. "Did something happen with him? Was he involved in the mall situation last year or close to the office when it was bombed?"

Buck shook his head. "Nope. He just finds us dangerous."

Haiden and Evan both scoffed their disapproval.

"So, what can we do about it?" Bexley shifted the rifle from her back to side. "I mean, does this mean we need to boost our position? Do some stories and generate a campaign?"

"Right now, we keep up with our training. I've asked Mayor Boist to keep us in the loop."

Danica chewed on her cheek. Why is the name Roltz familiar?

Her phone buzzed in her pocket. Kyra's name flashed.

"Dani?"

Her eyes jumped to Buck. "Yeah?"

"Let's get started. You and Haiden hit the course."

Frowning, she tossed her phone to Jeff and went to the beginning of the training course.

"Just don't shoot me, okay?" Haiden's crooked grin made her shake her head.

Focus, Danica. Just focus on your job.

The buzzer sounded, and she started through the mock doors of a simulated home. Roltz's name rolled around in her head, and she struggled to focus. Clearing the corner and the wall, she grimaced as she forgot to clear her left side. Entering the last room, she edged past the closet before turning and clearing it. It was a mistake that could cost her if this had been an actual event.

"What was that?" Buck blocked her path as she started back to the viewing box.

"Distraction?"

"What distracted you?"

"Phone call." Admitting her distraction ranged from the name Roltz to the shooting lesson with Haiden wasn't an admission that would help the situation. She pushed past him as Jeff stood with her phone, red faced. "What?"

"You need to get to Hico. Kyra was in a car accident."

"LET'S, uh, let's get back to it," Buck choked.

"What's that about?"

Jeff glanced at Evan. "He's concerned for Danica, and for Kyra, I'm sure."

"Evan, Bexley, let's go." Buck's gritty voice heaved out, and the two stepped into the course.

"Should you go?" Haiden sounded behind him.

"She'll be fine," Jeff mumbled.

"Not what I asked."

Jeff turned to Haiden. "Look, if Dani needs help, she'll let one of us know."

Haiden stared silently.

"You know we're just friends, right?"

Haiden nodded.

"We're practically family."

"Do you need to go?"

"No. Like I said, if Dani wants me there, she'll ask. She has a habit of taking on the world and handling it herself. Interfering would irritate her."

Haiden stifled a chuckle.

"I should ask what's going on with you, though." Jeff closed the distance between them. "Danica is a great friend, an amazing person. We all witnessed your dance at last year's gala, but now ... Is there a reason you've blown her off?"

Haiden's face went crimson. "Yes."

"It better be a good one," he mumbled.

"Jeff, you and Bexley." Buck's deep voice sounded.

Glaring at Haiden, Jeff turned to the course. Closing his eyes, he took a deep breath and cleared his mind, focused on the task. He was good at clearing his mind of distraction. It had helped him in more ways than one.

The buzzer sounded, and he pulled his gun free, stepped through the door, and began.

8

"You wanna explain that?"

Haiden took several deep breaths as he stared at Jeff's disappearing back, ignoring Evan's question.

"Hey."

"No."

Evan stepped in his line of sight. "I'm just curious. Why not?"

Haiden cut his eyes.

"You never answered me the other day."

"I have reasons."

Evan's jaw jumped. "Your dad?"

At the comment, Haiden rotated his head till his neck popped, then grabbed up his gun. "I'll be on the range." He took off out the back door.

As he walked to the box, his heart pounded. Evan had no idea what he was talking about. No one did. Just because Evan happened to see the scars on his back didn't give him a clue about the extent of the damage done.

Hanging the target, Haiden trod back to the box. He shouldered the rifle, exhaled out his frustration, and took aim. Emptying the clip, he flipped the safety and sat the rifle down.

Shooting was all he knew, all he could do. But it was enough to be wanted by the Army, so that's all he'd ever cared about.

Until he got out.

He held the target in his hand. A silver-dollar-sized hole bored out of the middle. His aim was still steady. Why couldn't he do so well in his life?

Thinking of Danica, he set the target down and pulled out his phone.

> Call me if you need anything. You know I'm here for you.

Even if he couldn't allow himself to go down that road with her, he still cared deeply. He could be there for her, no matter the circumstances.

> Thanks.

Letting out a breath, he slid the phone back in his pocket. Maybe one day the fear would dissipate. His future was in God's able hands. He'd just have to trust Him from now.

"Haiden?"

He turned. Buck stood at the door.

"Let's go. You're up."

Nodding, Haiden folded up the target and slung the rifle over his shoulder. He might not have a future in a personal sense. But he had a job—one he was still good at.

9

"The car's a wreck, Dani. She's lucky to be alive."

Danica paced the hospital hallway, speaking with Officer Riley about Kyra's accident.

"Do you know what happened? Was it her fault or someone else's?"

"Still looking it over. There are skid marks and possible paint transfer. The crime unit will take care of it and let me know how it all went down."

Nodding, she took a deep breath. Even though Kyra was in a coma with a broken leg, she was alive. "Where's my mom?"

"You don't know?"

She spun. "No. Where is she?"

Riley shrugged. "I don't know. I thought maybe she called you. She's not at the house, and I've tried her cell."

"No, no, no!" She frantically pulled her phone from her pocket and tried the house first, with no luck. Hanging up, she tried her mother's cell. It rolled over to voicemail. Pulling up Jeff's number, she paced while the phone rang.

"Hey, you okay?" Jeff sounded winded.

"No, I need you to trace my mom's cell."

"Why?"

"Just do it, please." She nervously paced.

"We're not at the office."

She groaned. "What about Buck?"

"He should have his tablet with him."

"Thanks." She hung up and called Buck.

"Is Kyra okay?"

"Can you trace my mom's cell?"

"Give me a sec."

She finally took a full breath. Buck was an action man. Do the job first, ask questions later. She didn't think she appreciated that more than she did right now.

"Her phone is on, but it shows her house."

"Oh no." She took off through the doors of the ER.

"Talk to me, Dani. What happened to Kyra? Do I need to come out there?"

"I ... I can't right now. I have to find Mom." She hung up and jumped into her car and backed out of the parking lot.

Flying down the back road to her childhood home, she pleaded, "God, please let her be okay. I can't handle both of them going down."

Slamming on her brakes about a mile from her house, she skidded across the gravel. A figure was walking toward her wearing jeans, a T-shirt, and a cowboy hat, but no shoes. The weather was cold, hovering in the forties. She put the car in park and jumped out.

"Mom?"

"Hey, Dani girl! I was hoping you would come by to visit today." Her mother had a huge grin on her face.

"Mom, get in the car, please."

"Why?"

"Mom, just ..." Danica took a calming breath before she lost it completely. "Mom, I need to get you back to the house and get your shoes. Kyra was in a car accident."

"Oh dear." Her mother paled, clutching her chest. "Is she okay?"

"She's not awake right now, and she broke her leg."

"Oh dear." Her mother kept repeating the phrase as she walked around the car and slid into the seat.

Once her mother was properly dressed in shoes and a coat, Danica drove back to town. She checked in with Kyra's doctor, then left Mom next to Kyra's bed and headed into the hallway to call her mother's doctor.

"Dr. Moore?"

"Danica? Is that you?"

She grinned at the woman's calm voice. "Yes, ma'am."

"Well, what are you up to, hun?"

"Actually, I need to speak to you about Mom."

"Is she okay?"

"I think her dementia is getting worse." She sighed and explained Kyra's accident and the state she found her mother in.

"I'm on my way down to the ER. You stay right there."

"You don't have to ..." The click confirmed the doctor had hung up.

She sighed and leaned against the wall, scrolling through the missed calls, ignoring the messages. Buck and Jeff had both called numerous times, but when she got to Haiden's text message, she smiled.

Even with their friendship teetering lately, he still texted to check on her. That was nice. She pocketed her cell phone and closed her eyes.

The smell of antiseptic and the clatter of carts jolted her memory. She straightened, blowing out a deep breath. Hospitals were miserable—the beds, the food, the constant noise and beeping ...

Unfisting her hands, she shook out her arms and paced. And waited.

JEFF SAT AT THE BOX, sighting in his target.

Not as proficient a shooter as Evan and Haiden, he had decided to put in some time where he needed it.

He took a deep breath and eased the trigger back.

The shrill of his phone broke his concentration. He groaned. Frowning at the missed bullseye, he snatched up the phone.

"Yeah?"

"Hey, man."

"Tony. What's going on?"

"I wanted to check on Dani and Kyra."

"How did you hear about it?"

"It's not like I still don't have friends there. Is Kyra okay?"

"Dani headed that way about an hour ago. She called about her mom but got off before I could get an answer about what happened."

The sound of a car door echoed through the line.

"Do you know?" Jeff questioned.

"What? No, I mean, someone called and said Kyra had an accident. I was going to offer Danica a ride, but then figured you or Buck took her."

"No. She took off like a shot. You can call her."

"It's fine. I'm sure I'll see her around. Talk to you later."

"Yeah, later." Jeff hung up and glanced down the range with a sigh. "I need some major work."

Jeff leaned against the box and scrolled through social media looking for this Roltz guy. He found several social media platforms the Roltz candidate was advertising on, along with commentary about police reform and restructuring.

After working as a profiler for ICE, Jeff had a pretty good idea about the power-driven man. Roltz, born into money and now a successful businessman—he was bound to have skeletons in his closet.

A quick search of the Roltz family showed several investigations. The IRS had audited them more than once during the past five years, suspecting tax avoidance and filing errors. There was also a corporate fraud case in the works for D&R Computing. Louis Roltz, the CEO, had been accused of misconduct.

How in the world could a guy like this get elected mayor?

10

"Well, as far as your mom is concerned, I think you should move home or move her in with you." Dr. Moore leaned toward Danica.

"What about nursing homes?" Danica's face heated. "Are there any around here that are specifically for patients with dementia?"

Dr. Moore smiled. "There are. I'll email you my top picks in the area, okay?"

She nodded, knowing the price tag would probably be too much.

"You ever think about moving home?"

Danica shook her head. "No. I enjoy my job in Dallas."

Dr. Moore narrowed her eyes. "How have *you* been, Danica?"

Not just a physician, Dr. Moore had been her therapist a long time ago.

"I'm good. But being here, this hospital ... it just brings up memories."

"Then you should talk about them."

Danica frowned. "I think we've talked it all out long ago, Dr. Moore."

"Maybe." Dr. Moore chuckled. "But as long as they keep

coming up, you need to keep talking. I'll be here for Kyra too. Once she wakes, I'll be glad to talk to her." She stood. "If you need anything, call me."

"Thanks."

When Dr. Moore left, Danica pulled her legs against her chest, protecting herself as her entire world was crashing once again.

"Dani?"

Tony Carlyle came sprinting down the hallway.

"Tony? What're you doing here?"

He collapsed in front of her and drew her into an awkward hug.

"I heard what happened. Is Kyra okay?"

She pushed herself free, ignoring Tony's frown as he backed off. "She'll be fine. Right now, they've put her in a medically induced coma. She hit her head, and there's some swelling. She has a broken leg too."

His eyes went wide. "Doesn't really sound as if she's okay, Dani."

"The doctor said the swelling is just something to keep an eye on, and her leg will heal. You should know that."

Tony sat next to her, wrapping an arm around her. "Yes, I know she'll heal. But it's still scary. What did the police say?"

"They're still investigating the scene." She stood from his reach. "But the way Riley explained what happened, it doesn't add up."

"You think this is drug related?"

Her face heated.

"I know you don't like to talk about it, but she had some issues, and if she owed someone, those guys can be scary."

Nodding along, Danica did her best to swallow the guilt laced with anger. It was her fault Kyra went down that road to begin with. Now it was all coming back.

"Dani?"

Forcing a smile, she focused back on Tony. "I appreciate you checking on me, but I'm okay. How did you get here so fast?"

"I was visiting my sister."

She inhaled sharply. "Oh? Is she doing well?"

Tony grinned. "Much better. We can sit and talk. It's been a wonderful turnaround that only took, what, ten years?"

"Fourteen," Dani mumbled. "Fourteen years."

After Buck found Danica and carried her to safety, her world collapsed. But Tony and his family were caught in the fallout. Although guilty, Tony had never left Danica's side or blamed her. He'd been a friend, just as concerned about her welfare as his own.. Even after his sister attempted suicide.

Letting out a sigh, he stood and pulled her in for a one more hug. "You're my good friend, and without you, things would've been worse. Okay?" He leaned back with a smile. "I'm serious."

"Thanks."

"You want me to sit here with you?"

She shook her head. "I need to find a place for Mom to stay until I can figure this out."

"Did you try Holden?"

"No, I guess I'll call them."

Pulling once more from his grasp, Danica walked down the hallway, phone in hand, and searched for the number. She needed to get out of this hospital—and town—as fast as possible. Swallowing the lump in her throat, she took a deep breath.

"Holden Homes, can I help you?"

"Yes, I need to see if you have a room available for my mother."

―――――

"It's fine, Buck. Really. Kyra will make a full recovery, and they've got a nice room set up for Mom."

"I should come down and see Kyra just in case."

"She's out for now. Besides, with everything else going on, you're needed there."

"You headed back?"

"I'm going to get Mom settled in, and then I'll head that way." Danica poked her head into the room to see her mom standing at the window. "I need to talk to you about long term homes for her. Her mind is getting worse."

"I'll help you however I can. You know that. But last time she saw me, she thought I was your dad, and she was upset."

Stepping back out into the hallway, Danica let out a sigh. "I know. I just might need some help deciding where to put Kyra. She won't stay at the house by herself."

"You're getting ahead of everything. One step at a time, Dani. Let Kyra get healed up and released, then we'll talk about where she can go. I've got room, and we have an extra room here if we need to."

Danica bit her lip. To keep personal issues in check, she and Jeff had kept their family connection with Buck quiet.

"Dani?"

"Yeah, I'm here." Snapping back to reality, Danica took in a breath. "Okay, we'll wait and figure it out later. Let me get Mom settled, and I'll head that way."

"Be careful."

"Always."

Hanging up, she slid the phone into her back pocket and stepped into the room. Her mother sat at the small table in the corner, her heavy coat wrapped in her arms.

"Let me hang that up, Mom."

"Thank you, dear."

Placing the coat in the closet, she turned back to her mother. "I'll be by in a few days to check in on you, okay?"

Her mother sat tentatively in the sterile room, a blank expression on her face.

"Mom?"

"Oh, I'll be fine." Her mother's wistful smile made Danica's heart ache.

With her sister in the hospital and no other family close by, this nursing home was the best option for her mother in her mental state.

"Dani?"

Danica turned to Molly, a nurse and a good friend from Dani's high school days.

"I've got dinner ready for your mom. You want to stay too?"

"That would be great. Thanks." She sat down at the table. "Let's eat dinner, and then it'll be time for bed."

"Wonderful. I'm starving."

Danica smiled as her mother sat down with her, chatting about old times that were brand new in her mother's eyes.

11

D anica let out a yawn as she strapped into her car.

It had taken only a few hours of eating and talking before her mother was ready to go to bed. She had changed and gotten into bed as if she were in her own home.

Leaving Mom at the nursing home wasn't the only option. Buck would gladly let her take some time, stay home, and let her sit with her mom and with Kyra. But the problem was, she needed to work. She needed some space and time to deal. Besides, being at home in the house alone ... it wouldn't work.

"You are so selfish," she mumbled to herself.

Turning onto the county road, she held her head. After years of therapy and struggle, she'd learned to forge ahead on her own. It was an independent streak she'd developed, and so far, it had protected her and kept her safe.

Gripping the steering wheel, Danica took a deep breath. Kyra had panic attacks, nightmares, and it was all Dania's fault. After all these years, it was still painfully clear that if she hadn't convinced Kyra to come with her to the run-down house across the field, Kyra would be just fine and probably some kind of amazing athlete by now.

Kyra had always been much more coordinated than her,

smart and competitive. But since that night, she'd become incapacitated by fear. Instead of being the star forward on the basketball team at twelve, Kyra gave up sports altogether and hid in her room in order to abide the panic attacks.

Bright lights in the rearview took Danica's attention. She sped up, hoping to avoid the glare. The roar of a truck engine made her glance up once more. The lights disappeared below her rearview.

"What in the world?"

A slight tap of the bumper and she jammed the accelerator to the floor. Defensive driving maneuvers flew through her mind, but her compact sedan against a truck wouldn't be a fair fight.

Ignoring another tap, she cut the wheel across traffic, turning onto another road. The truck rattled past, unable to make such a sharp turn. Swerving into the fast-food parking lot, she got out. The truck had vanished.

In a small town like hers, things like that didn't happen. And even if it did, she would recognize the truck. It was huge, bright red with a chrome grill and brush guard. But she had been gone a while. Maybe it was someone just playing a prank.

Blowing out a deep breath, she slid back inside and slammed the door shut.

AFTER A LATE DINNER, Jeff frowned at the article search results. He shook his head.

"What's wrong?" Buck sat next to him.

"That reporter. All the articles he's written were shady. He never gives specifics, just makes generalized comments on the inability for people to do their job. So far, I've not found one article where he actually made sense."

"He's protecting his source. Even with Roltz pushing buttons, it could be someone else feeding information. Did you call your guys? Find anything out?"

Jeff set down his phone. "Yeah, I called. They had no idea anything was wrong. One was there yesterday and mentioned the callout being delayed. They had to wait for Sutton to give them the green light."

"Sutton, huh?"

"I recognize that look." Jeff leaned back in his chair. "You know something."

"Nope."

"I don't believe you."

Buck chuckled. "I have a hunch, but I don't actually know anything."

"What is it?"

"There's something about Sutton that's pushing a button for me."

"From your overseas work?"

"Not work," Buck countered. "But there's something about him. I can't put my finger on it. I did some background on him, and he's had a great career as an officer. Stand-up guy with a few commendations in his file, including the Rookie of the Year back when he was a beat cop."

"Military?"

Buck shook his head.

"Then where could you know him from? Where did he grow up?"

"That's the thing. I couldn't go back to his high school days. The trail disappears."

"A cop without a history? That doesn't make sense. They have thorough background checks."

"Now you know why I don't know anything."

Jeff chuckled as his phone vibrated. Sutton's name flashed across the screen.

"Powers."

"We've got a possible hostage situation. Men with guns reported at a strip mall."

Jeff stood and snapped his fingers at the others in the living room. "Text me the coordinates and details."

"Get there fast. We've sent in officers but haven't heard anything."

"On our way." Jeff glanced down as the text came through. "Load up. We've got to hurry. Possible officer-involved shooting. Sutton says they haven't had contact since their officers arrived."

"Dani just called. Send her the address, and she'll meet us there." Bexley nodded and rushed past to the equipment room.

Jeff loaded the address into everyone's contact number and snatched his coat from the dining room chair.

God, keep us safe and let those officers be all right.

12

"Move to the secondary location."

Evan's gritty voice in her ear, Danica sprinted from her spot on the ground. Crouching behind the large SUV parked in the front of the lot, she searched the area.

"Where are the police?" she asked as Buck came in behind her.

"I've not had a call. Neither has Jeff," he answered.

Haiden set up outside on top of the team's SUV. "Two shooters." His low voice echoed in her earpiece. "One at the southeast corner entry, the other at the back door. Front entry has a large caliber weapon, possible AR. Proceed with caution."

"No one advance," Buck ordered. "We're not to advance until the police get here."

"I see a police cruiser at the back. Both doors are open," Bexley announced through the coms. "No blood, but there are bullet holes in the side."

"Stand down. Take cover and wait. Until we hear threats against any hostages, we need to wait for the police to arrive."

Buck's face turned crimson under his hat and *shemagh* covering his neck.

"Haiden? You see hostages?" Evan's voice growled from her right as he hid behind a dump trailer filled with debris.

"No, no visual."

"Maybe they were able to retreat," she said.

"Then we would've seen them on the way in. Something's not right," Buck responded.

"This place is empty. Why're they here?"

Danica glanced around the barely finished strip mall that contained four storefronts. The glass still had plastic taped across to protect it and fresh paint signs on the door. Even she could see all the way through the building with the large windows, the outdoor lights keeping the area lit up. The men inside weren't even trying to hide.

"What could these guys want here, and why would they bring weapons like an AR?"

"If this is a new building, could have copper, electronics, equipment or computers ready for set up," Buck whispered.

"Just got a text from Sutton. One minute out." Jeff informed them.

Why would the police not come quicker when there was no communication with their own officers?

"Got movement out the back—"

"Bexley?" Evan's voice cut off Haiden. "Bex?" he hissed.

"It's called hiding and being quiet," Bexley shot back. "Two guys in masks just left in an old truck that was sitting in the field."

"Then they entered from the back instead of the front. Is that why the police cruiser was in the back?" Danica asked.

Buck shrugged as he straightened. "I don't know. But let's clear it. Find those officers."

"You don't want us to track those men down?" Haiden mumbled.

"No. Clear the building first."

Danica and Evan followed Buck to the door. On his count, Evan kicked the door, and they made entry.

"Oh no," she whispered.

Two officers were face down on the ground, hands bound at their backs, unmoving, with blood pooling on the floor.

13

"Get some help in here!"

She rushed to the scene and checked for pulses. "They're alive," she yelled, cutting them loose. "Call an ambulance!"

Assessing their injuries, both were unconscious from major hits to the head, which caused the massive bleeding. Buck knelt next to her and used his scarf to put pressure on one of the wounds.

"Anyone else?" She glanced up, and Buck shook his head.

"Evan and Haiden are finishing up the other stores. Bexley's getting us some help," he mumbled as sirens echoed outside.

Gently pressing on the other officer's head, she kept her other fingers at his throat, monitoring his pulse.

"You see any other injuries?" she asked.

"No. I guess the guys just wanted to rob the place, not kill anyone."

"What happened?" A paramedic entered the room, two others on her heels with a gurney.

"Head injury, unconscious, but pulse is strong." Danica stood out of the way as the paramedics took over.

"Let's go, Dani." Buck led her from the building, meeting

Haiden and Bexley at the back of the building. "No one says a word." Buck's gray eyes stared at each of them.

She nodded with a frown as Buck left.

"Why did he say that?" Bexley whispered.

"The police will look to place blame. We got here and should've advanced. Buck told us to wait."

Danica glared at Haiden. "We didn't see the hostages. We had no idea what was inside."

Haiden shrugged as he hugged the rifle across his chest. "It won't matter. Two of their own are injured."

"They weren't shot."

"That's a good thing," Danica quipped to Bexley.

Her eyebrows knitted together. "No, I mean, they weren't shot. The cruiser has bullet holes as if someone let an AR go. Yet, it doesn't look like the officers even received a nick."

Glancing at the beat-up cruiser, the glass remained untouched, but the body of the car was riddled with holes.

Danica's jaw ached as she watched Buck interact with a red-faced Sutton.

"Where were you?" Sutton shouted.

Buck stood silently.

"Those are our men. Why didn't you advance? Or at least stop the assailants from leaving?"

"We cleared the buildings." Buck nodded to the large strip mall. "Our concern was for your men, not the guys who stopped them."

"Then you would've been in here sooner." Sutton stormed off.

Haiden touched Danica's shoulder. "Don't do it."

"Do what?"

"You want to save him. He doesn't need saving. He's doing what he needs to do to keep the peace. Once they calm down, things will be better."

She bit the inside of her lip. How could Haiden see right through her?

As she shifted her stance, his hand held her back, gently rubbing up and down. Walking away would be the right thing to do. After all, falling all over herself for a guy who didn't want more from her would be devastating. She enjoyed that support, that comfort of Haiden at her back. Especially after today.

"We need to get back to the office." Jeff walked up.

"What's wrong now?"

"That reporter from earlier has help, and we need to figure out where to go from here. This will be all over social media within the hour."

Haiden's arm went around Danica's waist, and he guided her to the SUV.

"Where's Buck?" Evan's eyes dropped to her side as Haiden held on.

"He's trying to smooth things over with the police." Danica set the gear in the back.

She leaned against the door and held her head.

"Dani? Everyone okay?"

She nodded but couldn't hold back any longer. Haiden wrapped her up in a hug, and she held on. Seeing her sister in the hospital and her mother's confusion taking over, this job had become her home. If it fell apart, too, where would she go?

———————

"Is Kyra okay?"

Danica nodded to Jeff as she collapsed on the couch. "She's going to be okay. They have her in an induced coma while she heals."

Bexley sat down next to her. "Why're you here at work? Why didn't you stay there?"

"There's nothing I can do. The doctor thinks she'll be out for a while, and she's stable. I would rather be here." She wrinkled her nose, realizing that sounded terrible. "I mean, I just need to be busy."

Bexley patted her leg. "I get it."

Haiden sat down on the other side, his arm going behind her on the back of the couch.

"Did Buck have a conversation with this Roltz guy?"

"No." Jeff shook his head. "But the press has started a campaign targeting us." He opened his phone and held it out to her.

Danica snatched it up and read the headline. "Private SWAT team off book? What does that mean?"

"The last two callouts, we went in without police aiding us. It's making news. Even though things went smoothly." Jeff shrugged. "Except for today, which will be all over the news tonight. We can only hope they leave our name out of it."

"This says the TRT uses their extensive field training to step in and push out law enforcement." Danica glanced up with a frown. "Is that what your friends are telling you?"

"No." Jeff took the offered phone back. "My guys don't know where this is coming from. But after today's two injured officers, we're going to get hit hard. It's not just about Roltz now."

Buck walked in from the back and took a seat in the living room.

"We need to figure out why Roltz has a beef with us. Fast." Evan's gravelly voice echoed in the room. "Then we need to get it out there about the officers and what happened today. Otherwise, we'll be the bad guys in all this."

"I've been informed by Captain DeSalis that no comment about us will be made until the entire situation is resolved. The officers are at the hospital. They're waiting for them to wake up," Buck said.

Danica leaned back as the conversation flowed around her. That name Roltz was familiar, but so far, she still couldn't place it.

"From what I've found, Martin Roltz is a philanthropist who lives here in Dallas and gives to a lot of small-town businesses. He's received awards and recognition for helping local businesses achieve national success." Jeff furrowed his brows at his phone. "Then, his son Louis became successor to the family business and now controls the assets. He's put in a bid to run for mayor. This article says he's a true businessman who knows how to negotiate and make cuts in order to make businesses successful."

"Let me check the donor list." Buck countered. "Martin's name sounds familiar."

"Oh, my." Danica's face heated. The memory of Louis Roltz spinning her around on the dance floor permeated her brain. Her stomach flipped.

"What's wrong?" Bexley bumped her shoulder.

"I remember." Danica stared up at Buck. "He was at the gala. He asked me to dance and commented on the fact our group was about to be belly up in financial debt. He mentioned his father donating and didn't seem too happy about it."

"M.R. Investments," Buck said.

"What?"

Buck stood. "M.R. Investments LLC gave us the majority of our start-up capital. It's owned by Martin. That's why his name was so familiar. He uses the LLC to pay out his charitable donations. Without that, we wouldn't have this team. I spoke to him years ago, and he wanted this group up and running— donated over half the cost when I first started it. I work primarily with his fund manager, Christian Toller."

"So, why would his son want to dismantle us?" Danica frowned.

"It's cutting into his wealth." Jeff leaned over, showing her the article on his phone. "This says Martin is in poor health, and Louis is ready to take over. Louis is also facing a few legal issues, and I'm sure he's looking to keep as much money in the bank as possible."

"Martin never comes to the gala. I haven't spoken directly to him in years," Buck muttered.

"You would think a guy running for mayor would use the fact his father helps protect the city by funding our group. That's a big point to make in the safety of the city and its residents." Evan glared at Danica. "So you ticked him off?"

"Of course not. We danced. He made his comments, and I told him we were credited with the capture of a known terrorist."

"You sure you didn't say anything?"

Danica frowned at a glowering Haiden. "Look, I didn't say anything negative. He was the one being hateful. I told him to have a nice evening and left. He wasn't thrilled with his father donating to us, and then with the explosion and everything, he acted like we were a lost cause."

Bexley let out a sigh.

"It's not your fault." Evan wrapped an arm around Bexley's shoulder.

"It feels like it," Bexley muttered.

"Arlo was coming after you, no matter what. At least it was here and there weren't any civilian casualties."

Danica nodded and patted Bexley's leg. "Evan's right. This isn't your fault. We did our job and stopped a terrorist. I have a feeling this Louis guy would come after us, no matter what."

"But now he has ammo."

"I have an idea." Jeff stood and motioned to Bexley. "Come on. I think we can combat this bad press."

Bexley and Evan followed Jeff to the back office.

"Tell me what else is going on. Kyra?"

Danica turned to Buck. "You heard it. The hospital will call with any changes in Kyra's condition, and Mom is good." Her eyes cut to Haiden, then back to Buck. "What do we need to do in the meantime?"

"Let's see what Jeff has planned." Buck gave her a wink and stood, heading to the back office as well.

Haiden's arm went around her shoulders. "You should be at home with your sister."

She shrugged, turning her phone over and over on her knee. "No. I can't just sit in the hospital."

"Dani." He squeezed her shoulder.

Standing, she tried to push past when he stood, but he took hold of her hand.

"Talk to me."

Her heart pulled as she stared into his big green eyes. "Haiden, you have your stuff, and I have mine. Let's just let it go."

"What if I want ... want to help?"

She sighed. "I appreciate you wanting to help. But I ... things are really complicated, and I don't think—"

"I can help." His Adam's apple bobbed.

Getting this close to Haiden was a dangerous game. As much as she wanted to just fall into his arms and let him take the weight for a moment, it was something she couldn't do.

Straining to shift her focus, she glanced down at his hand holding hers. "We should leave it, okay? No sense in getting caught up—"

"Caught up in what?"

Her eyes jumped to his as he stepped closer.

"You can talk to me," he whispered. "Any time, Dani."

"Thanks," she mumbled as she pulled from his grip and headed to Buck's office.

Collapsing in the chair, she let out a slow breath.

"You, okay?"

She shrugged as her body shuddered. Haiden was getting awfully close for someone who just wanted to remain friends.

"Tell me what's really going on."

Looking at her uncle, she shook her head as memories flooded her mind.

"You having nightmares again?"

"No."

Not yet.

"Then talk."

"I'm just worried about what I'm going to do with Mom and then Kyra. Once Kyra heals, she won't stay in the house alone ..."

The shrill ring of her phone made her groan. She pulled it out. "Hello?"

"Hey, Dani."

"Officer Riley? What's wrong?"

"I'm just calling to let you know that the crime unit has an estimated guess of what happened today. They've not put in the paperwork, but I wanted to give you a heads up."

She sat up, her heart racing. "Okay?"

"It looks like she was run off the road."

"What? By whom?"

"We don't know. There were skid marks and paint transfer on the driver's side. Someone hit her pretty hard to throw her into the tree."

Standing, Danica paced. "But ... I mean, who would do something like that? Kyra has no enemies."

"We're looking through traffic footage to see if we can determine whether or not someone was following her through town. Based on the height of the damage, a large truck hit her."

She paused. "A red truck?"

"Nope. Based on paint transfer, white."

Frowning, she turned to see Buck standing at the desk, his arms crossed. "Thanks for calling me. Let me know if you figure something out."

"I sure will. Take care."

"Thanks." She hung up.

"What did Riley have to say?"

Danica repeated her conversation with Officer Riley back to Buck.

"She was targeted?"

Danica shrugged and slunk into the chair. "I can't believe this. No one would target Kyra."

Buck sat beside her and took her hand. "Is she using again?"

Shaking her head, Danica wiped the tears forming in her eyes. Kyra had taken to drug use a few years after the incident. It wasn't like Danica hadn't thought of that as well. Exhausted from no sleep and in constant fear—narcotics were an easy way to escape. But she had been older and maybe just a little wiser than Kyra.

"She's not used in forever. I mean, I don't think she has."

"Why else would someone go after her? Kyra doesn't make enemies. But if she's using ... It wouldn't take much for them to come after her."

"I talked to her this morning. She was fine, said she had an interview for a new job," Danica said. "I have a hard time believing she was on anything."

"Maybe you should go back home, take care of your mom and Kyra."

"We'll see." Pushing herself to stand, she headed for the door.

"Why did you ask about a red truck?"

She shrugged. "Just wondered."

Trudging upstairs, she let out a sigh. The incident with the red truck was just some kid thinking she was someone else. No need to involve Buck.

Fighting tears, Danica collapsed in her bed. It was almost midnight, and she needed sleep. Flashes of a dirt grave made her flinch. The smell of damp earth and a burning sensation ate at her left shoulder.

Please God, take away these nightmares.

14

Haiden slammed down the last set of weights, then grabbed a towel.

Pacing the room, he snatched up a water bottle and sucked down what he could. After being shaken awake by dreams, he decided on an early workout. Dani's face flashed through his mind, and all he wanted to do was help fix whatever was going on that she didn't want to talk about.

Every time he considered a relationship with her, all he could think of was his father.

You are pathetic!

That voice echoed in his head. Father's words somehow still took over his thoughts. Haiden hated it. He had beaten on and hurt everyone he came into contact with, including Mom and a string of girlfriends who had always left with a police escort.

Haiden quickly made his way down the hall to shower. He ignored the burning sensation in his arms and back from pushing the weights too hard. Closing his eyes and leaning against the tile, he stopped himself from punching the wall. He wouldn't hit anything. Ever. He would not be his father. There were times he'd used his fists as a child and had always regretted it.

The taught skin on his back pulled as he moved his arms and

shoulders, but it was worth it. Shielding Dani from the blast and taking the glass that would've hurt her was the only thing he could do during the explosion to keep her safe.

After drying, he came into his bedroom and heard his phone.

"Hello?"

"Haiden."

"Mom?"

"I need you to meet me at the hospital."

"Wh-what? Are you okay? What happened?"

"I'm fine. I just need you to come see me."

His jaw clenched. "Yeah, o-okay. Which one?"

"It's the one you were at last year. Baylor something?"

How did she know about that?

"I'll be there in a minute."

"Wonderful. Be careful, dear."

He paused at the comment. "Okay."

Tossing the phone on the bed, he stared at it for a moment. Why was his mom at the hospital? And how did she know he'd been there last year?

JEFF SAT BACK on the couch as Lonnie, his reporter friend from college, finished up her interview of Bexley.

"I really appreciate you re-living all of that. I know it wasn't easy."

Bexley shrugged. "It's in the past, and so far, I think things have turned out for the best."

"Sounds like it." Lonnie turned to him. "What about you?"

Jeff sat down his coffee with a frown. "What about me?"

"You gonna let me interview you?"

"Not a chance." He stood and motioned her to the door. "That wasn't part of the deal. I'll see about the others and get some time set up when you're free."

"Jeff, it would be a good idea to do a group story here. Stir up some public interest."

"Not sure it's the right kind of interest."

Lonnie sighed as she steeled him with a glare. "You hold on to things too long."

Jeff frowned.

"If you'd just compartmentalize like you say you do so well, maybe things would work out with someone else." She smiled big, but Jeff only nodded.

"Thanks for the help. I'll see what I can do about either comments from the others or maybe another interview."

Lonnie sighed. "Okay, but one of these days, I'm going to stop being interested."

Jeff closed the door behind her and saw Bexley smirking. "What?"

"You want to explain what that was about?"

"What *what* was about?" He pushed past her to the living area.

She followed him. "Come on, Jeff. She was hitting on you, and you completely ignored her."

"The reporter?" Evan leaned into the island as Jeff grabbed a water bottle. "Is there a reason you didn't take the bait?"

Taking a long drink, Jeff mulled the right answer. "I've known Lonnie forever. She's not my type."

Evan chuckled as Jeff hurried down the hallway to his room.

Pacing the area, Jeff let out a sigh. Lonnie was a good friend, a really attractive, nice friend. But she had been Meline's good friend as well. Although they were both older and much more mature now, it was odd for Lonnie to hit on him.

"Hey."

Haiden's voice had him turn.

"Yeah?"

"I've got to run an errand. But I've got my things. Call if you need me."

Jeff frowned. "We're a little shorthanded with Sergio out."

Haiden stood there staring, his jaw taut.

"Fine. If something comes up, I'll call you. Everything all right?"

"I guess I'm about to find out." Haiden turned and took off down the hallway.

Haiden lived at the office full time, like they all did. He occasionally took his weekend off, but he was here and ready for callouts, even if it wasn't his rotation.

Danica walked into the hallway just as the garage door shut. "Where's Haiden going?"

"I'm not sure. Did he say anything to you?"

She shook her head, her cheeks turning pink.

"You sure you guys are okay?"

"We're fine. But Bex mentioned an attractive reporter being here earlier. Do *you* want to explain?"

He huffed and stepped back into his room. "Nothing to explain. I'll talk to you later."

Slamming the door in Dani's face reminded of him of times past, practically growing up in her home with her mother and sister. Memories flooded, and he let out a sigh.

"Forget the past," he mumbled, and sat down at his computer.

He had work to do, and it started with stopping the social media outcry against their department.

15

H aiden stepped into the Dallas campus of Baylor University Hospital. A blast of cool air hit his face as the hospital doors closed behind him.

"Haiden."

"Hi, Mom." He embraced her for only a second, then waited for her to release him.

"I'm so glad you came."

"Wh-what's going on? Why am I here?"

She tugged on his arm. "Let's go upstairs."

Following in silence, he leaned against the back of the small elevator, attempting to ease the pounding in his chest.

Stepping off the elevator, the signs pointed out "Cancer Center."

He pulled her to the side. "Tell me wh-what's going on. Now."

"Well, I ..." she trailed off as she wiped the tears rolling down her cheek.

"Are you o-okay?"

"I'm fine. Really." She nodded to the family waiting room. "Let's sit for a minute."

Easing down to the chair, she let out a haggard breath.

"Mom. Why am I here?"

"It's your father. He's sick."

Haiden's fists clenched, and he paced the small room. "I don't w-want to see him."

"Haiden."

"Wh-why're you here? After what he did to you, t-to us."

His mother dabbed her eyes with a tissue and leaned back in her chair. She patted the seat next to her. "Sit down. Please."

Perching on the edge of the chair, Haiden leaned over his knees.

"There are some treatments, but he's refusing them all right now. I think he believes he has to suffer and doesn't deserve to be healed."

He wanted to agree, but held back his comment. "How bad?"

"His liver is failing, has been for the past several years. It started out as cirrhosis. Now they think it's cancer. The doctor says he's at a point of no return. Right now, treatment might not save him, but might prolong his life. But ... he's waited, so ... I don't know."

She wiped her face, and Haiden couldn't believe his mother could sit here and cry for the man. His father had beaten her so badly so many times, berated her, and destroyed her life. And yet, she was obviously taking care of him now.

"Why are you doing this?" He clenched his jaw, his face on fire.

"Because I know he's different. He's more like the man I married all those years ago before he started drinking. You know, he wasn't always a monster. Until you were five or six, he was a wonderful person and father. He loved us both more than anything. Then one day, he came home, and he was different. Then it got worse and worse." She wiped her face and stood.

"We started talking, just phone calls, six years ago. He reached out to me, and I immediately saw the change in him. Last year, he moved into the guest room above the garage and has helped take care of the house. We talk, we eat together ...

this past year we've even laughed together. He'll never be the man he was when we married, but this is as close as it will get. I care for him. I just want you to see the man your father used to be, the man he could've become."

He swallowed and nodded, not sure if he could really see anything other than the man he'd known as a child.

"Haiden, if you were to ask your father to get the help he needs—"

"No." He shook his head and stood, pacing.

"But he's not the same."

"It's his choice."

"It doesn't have to be."

"How long did it take you to forgive him?"

She sighed. Hopefully, she understood. He couldn't just suddenly be okay with what had happened, with the devastation his father caused in his life, just because he was sick and hurting.

"Would you please just go see him?"

Pausing, Haiden surveyed his mother. She had always been small and fragile. He'd always thought his father had done that to her.

"Please. It would mean the world to him if you'd just talk to him. Let him see you."

Attempting to swallow the lump in his throat, Haiden nodded.

His mother stood and led him down the dull corridor to one of the rooms on the right. Taking a deep breath, he followed her inside.

His father lay in the large hospital bed with his eyes closed.

"Curtis?"

The man's eyes opened. Red and bulging, it didn't take long before he centered on Haiden.

"You ... you came," he whispered.

Haiden crossed his arms and stood at the door, unable to move closer.

"I'll be outside." His mother patted his arm and left the room.

His father sat up in the bed, swinging his legs to the side with a grunt. Wearing sweats and a hospital ID bracelet, his yellow skin sagged around his neck, his body frail. "I, I wanted to talk to you last time, Haiden."

Haiden clenched his jaw.

"Last year, when I came to the hospital after your accident ..."

"I told you, I don't w-want to ... to hear it." He could feel his heartbeat pounding in his ears.

"Haiden, we could've lost you."

"That was a fifty-fifty chance every ... every day growing up."

"Haiden." His father's voice went stern, and Haiden frowned.

"Don't even think about it da ... dad."

"Please. I need you to listen."

Haiden's breathing picked up. He fisted his hands under his crossed arms.

He fell asleep every night praying God would take his father away and that he would find a home with parents who loved him. Not his father nor another of mother's boyfriends who beat him unconscious for being too loud or stupid.

"I know you don't care, Haiden. I know I don't deserve for you to listen to what I have to say. But I need to say it. I'm sorry. I can't take back who I was, but I can show you who I am now."

Haiden scoffed. "W-who you are now?" He found himself with that same anger he had as a child.

"Do it." His father stepped up to him. Years of alcohol abuse had yellowed his skin. "I deserve it. I know you want to hit me. You've always wanted to hit me. I deserve nothing less."

Haiden's body shook as his father stood there, weak and vulnerable. For the first time in his life, he was the one who could take charge, who had the power on his side to stand up for himself and his mother. But he couldn't do it.

"If I hit you, I-I become just like you."

"You could never become like me. You're better than me. You could never be as terrible as I was. I'm not him anymore. God took it away, my hate, my anger, my ... my sin."

"You can't be saved," Haiden hissed, furious, thinking his father could be forgiven for what he had done.

"I am. It doesn't make me right or better. But I can stand here and tell you, I don't have that in me anymore. I haven't had a drink in seven years, and I don't want to drink. I don't want to be angry. I was wrong, and I'm so sorry."

"W-what do you want me to say?"

"Nothing. I don't want you to say anything." His father took a shaky breath. "I just want you to know that I was wrong, and I'm sorry, and that none of it was your fault. I was the problem. And I'm so proud that you have become such an amazing man without my help."

Haiden stared blankly at his father, unsure of what to do or say. "I-I have to go."

Turning from the room, Haiden ignored his mother's voice as he pushed through the stairwell door and raced down the steps.

16

"I just wanted to check on you."

Danica nodded and held the office door for Tony. "You didn't have to come by."

Tony shrugged as he walked past. "You looked pretty upset the other day. Do you need anything?"

She sighed and took a seat on the couch. "I think everything's okay right now. No update from the hospital, and my mom is doing just fine at the nursing home."

"You know, Buck would let you be there for them."

"I know. But there's nothing I can do. Sitting around and waiting isn't my strong suit."

Tony chuckled. "You think I don't know that?"

She forced a smile.

He sat next to her. "Look, I don't have to show up at the hospital until later tonight. You want to go somewhere? Out to eat?"

She leaned forward on her knees. "We've got some PR issues, and Buck's been adamant that we keep low profiles."

"And going out is going to put you in the middle of a social media storm? Come on, let's go get something."

"We're going out?" Jeff walked through the door of his room, a grin on his face.

"What're you smiling about?"

"I think my plan is working out."

She huffed.

"What plan? What's going on?" Tony rubbed Danica's back, his gaze fixed on Jeff.

"After reading that story the other day on our unwillingness to work with law enforcement and how reckless we are, I became pro-active."

"Does this have anything to do with the reporter friend you wouldn't tell me about?" She shifted, pulling away from Tony's contact.

"Yes. She's a friend from college, and I asked if she'd write an article about what happened, highlighting our backgrounds. Besides Haiden and Evan, we're all former civil servants, and even the military background from those guys and Buck would be a good angle."

"Angle? You really think Buck wants to resort to using his service as an angle?"

Jeff rolled his eyes at her. "Okay, angle is a bad choice of words. But you know what I mean. We're all trained in service. It's what we do. She's already sent me a writeup for tomorrow's news release, and it's great."

"What PR issues?"

"A guy named Louis Roltz has made it clear he's not a supporter."

Tony frowned. "The guy running for mayor? What's he got to do with this?"

"He's been talking about change that would effectively put us out of business. Lately, things have been strange with work. The police not showing up or showing late. Headlines saying we're some sort of vigilante justice." Danica stood and paced. "But the police we do work with seem just fine with us being there for backup. It doesn't make sense."

"You off today?"

Tony shook his head at Jeff's question. "No. My shift starts at 8."

"Late shift. Yikes." Jeff winced.

Tony had overcome so much in his life, even making it through nursing school. He was an RN at the local hospital and had been there last year when Haiden was healing.

"Hey, my phone's dead." Tony held out the blackened screen. "Can I borrow yours to double check my schedule?"

"Yeah." Danica handed him her phone.

Tony sighed. "Yep. Eight to seven forty-five. Then back at one."

"Man, I don't know how you do those hours."

Jeff and Tony's voices droned into the background as she breathed through the nervousness running through her veins. She had barely slept last night—nightmare after nightmare bolting her into the darkness as she jumped from her bed several times.

"Dani?"

Her gaze cut between the two men. "I'm sorry. What?"

"We're going to go get pizza."

"Oh, I'm not really hungry."

The slam of a door caught her attention, and Haiden entered from the front, red-faced.

"You okay?"

His eyes centered on Tony sitting next to her before finally cutting toward her. "Yeah," he answered.

"Hey, man. You look good."

Haiden shot a glare to Tony and marched through the room.

"You want to go eat with us?" Jeff called as Haiden entered the hallway.

"No."

"Is he always so—"

"Yes," she and Jeff replied in unison.

Tony chuckled. "Okay then. You ready?"

"You two go ahead. I'm not in the mood to get out."

"Come on. It'll make you feel better."

She frowned up at Tony. "I just want to sit around. Thanks for the invite."

Tony's jaw clenched. He gave a nod. "Let's go, Jeff."

"I'll bring you a slice." Jeff winked as he headed out the front door with Tony.

Danica leaned back on the couch, holding the remote in her hand. She wondered what had Haiden so upset. He rarely showed so much emotion.

Refraining from asking if he was okay, she turned on the TV. She grabbed her phone from the ottoman where Tony had left it and texted instead.

I'm watching a movie if you want to come join.

Bubbles popped up and down on the screen.

No, thanks. Need some space.

Frowning, she tossed the phone back on the couch. Of course, he wanted space.

Buck walked in.

"Where's Jeff?"

"He and Tony just went out for lunch."

"Tony? Since when?"

She shrugged and stared blankly at the TV screen. "He saw me at the hospital yesterday and came by to check on me."

"Why was he there?"

"He said he was visiting his sister and heard the news."

Buck sat next to her. Leaning her head on his shoulder, she sighed.

"It'll get better."

"When? I think you've been saying that for fourteen years."

"You don't think it's better than back then?" He nudged her side. "You've become an amazing field operator, and you do your job every day, despite what you're shouldering."

She sat up. "I know, I'm just whining."

"No problem dealing, Dani. Now you gotta get up and live your life. I've always told you it's okay to take time and deal. You need more time, let me know."

"I'm fine," she mumbled.

Her phone vibrated. "Hello?"

"Dani?"

Her mouth dropped. "Mom? Are you okay?"

"Of course, dear. I was wondering if you would stop by the store for me."

Why did it sound as if her mom was at home and not at the nursing home?

"Mom, where are you?"

"I'm at home. Where else would I be?"

"You're ... you're at home?" She stood and took off for her room. "Mom, what do you need from the store? I'll bring it to you."

"Just some milk and some eggs. I have an entire list written out. For some reason, we have nothing in the house."

"Okay, I'm leaving work right now, but I might be about an hour, okay?"

"I'll be here."

"Yes, stay inside. The weather is bad, so stay inside."

"I will, dear. See you in a bit."

She hung up and threw some things in a duffle bag. Running to the bathroom, she pulled her makeup bag out and filled it quickly, then came to her bedroom.

Buck entered. "What's going on?"

"Mom somehow got out of the nursing home. I'm headed that way. I'll call Riley and see if he'll sit in the driveway and make sure she doesn't go anywhere until I get there."

Dani zipped her bag. Buck snatched it off the bed for her as she grabbed her extra boots and her charger from the nightstand.

Racing down the steps, she paused. Haiden stood at the back door.

"I'll take you home."

"No, you stay here. I'll be fine." She pushed past him toward the garage.

Haiden's Jeep was parked inside, and Buck was loading her bag into the back seat.

"What? What're you doing?"

"Haiden offered to drive you home."

"No. I mean, I can drive."

"Dani, you're not taking off like you did last time. Driving upset and worried isn't safe. Either he drives you, or I will."

She groaned and yanked open the passenger side door of the Jeep.

The two men moved to the back of the Jeep before Haiden slide into the driver's seat.

"Why are you doing this, and how did you get Buck to agree?"

"He's worried about you. So am I." He backed out without another word.

She punched Riley's name into her phone contacts. "Hey Riley, can you do me a favor?"

"I can try. What's going on?"

Danica quickly brought him up to speed about her mother.

"Will do. Be careful. Out here we've got some freezing temps headed this way. Might get bad."

"Great. Thanks for the heads up." She hung up and sighed.

"Which way?"

"North. We're going to Hico."

He nodded and changed lanes as the Jeep sped down the interstate.

"The sheriff says there's a chance of some ice with the rain and freezing temps."

"Good thing I'm driving. Your car ... it wouldn't make it."

She frowned as a smirk fell across his face.

17

The shrill of Danica's phone shattered the uncomfortable silence in the car. "Hello?"

"Danica? Oh, thank goodness. I'm so sorry to call you, but I can't find your mother."

"It's okay, Molly. She called me from home. Officer Riley is monitoring her until I get there."

"I'm so sorry. I came back from lunch and I ... I couldn't find her."

"Don't worry about it. I'm sure she found a ride. I'm headed there now."

"Oh, Danica," Molly's voice trembled.

"It's fine. I'll be there sometime tomorrow for her things."

"Okay. I'll get everything together. See you tomorrow."

"Bye." She blew out a sigh and dropped her phone into the cup holder.

Danica leaned back into the seat, closing her eyes and allowing her irritation with Buck's bushwhacking to ease.

"You haven't mentioned your sister."

Her eyes opened and cut to Haiden, his focus completely on the road.

"She's still out. Not much to say."

"You two get along?"

She sighed. "Most of the time. Things have been hard for her …"

"I wouldn't know. I don't have any siblings." He cleared his throat.

"You looked upset earlier. Is everything all right?"

He frowned. "Not really. There's some stuff."

The silence lingered until they entered the town. She gave him directions to the house and sighed with relief when she saw Riley sitting on the porch with her mother.

"There you are, Dani girl!"

She grinned as she got out and gave her mother a hug.

"Did you know Riley here is a grandpa now? He was showing me pictures of his beautiful granddaughter."

"Yes, I know, Mom." She gripped her mother's hand and nodded to Riley with a smile.

"And you brought a friend."

Haiden walked up behind her, carrying her duffle bag.

"Oh, this is Haiden. I work with him."

"It's so nice to meet one of Dani's co-workers. Please, come inside."

She waved to Riley as her mother gripped Haiden's arm, pulling him along. Danica tried to muffle her laughter when Haiden flushed.

Once inside, she found Haiden grinning as he listened to her mother point out her senior pictures that hung on the wall. Good grief. If he smiled like that all the time, he would find more than one woman's attention.

"Mom, have a seat a minute." She pulled her mother to the couch and sat next to her.

"Did you ask your friend if he wanted something to drink?"

"I'm fine, thanks." He crossed his arms and leaned against a wall.

"Where were you this morning?" She bent close to her mother, trying to get her attention.

"Oh, I meant to tell you. I guess I found a ride to the nursing home to see Tilly, but they told me she was no longer there. So then, I started walking to the house, and my friend Carley found me. Do you remember Carley?"

"From church?"

She nodded. "Anyway, she said she would give me a ride home." Her mother sat back in her seat. Pride gleamed in her eyes.

"I'm glad you made it okay."

"I would make us dinner, but I have nothing to bake with. It's like our pantry and the fridge were completely emptied."

She forced a smile. "I guess I've gotten behind on keeping up with the groceries."

"Well, it doesn't matter. Let's go out to dinner." Her mother stood and headed to the stairwell.

"Mom, I don't think we—"

"Oh, nonsense. I would love to sit and chat with this handsome man you brought with you."

Danica's face heated as her mother patted Haiden on the shoulder before slowly making her way upstairs.

After her mother entered her room, Dani sighed and turned her focus to Haiden. "Look, you can go. I'll have Jeff come get me later. With Sergio out and Bexley training, Buck will need everyone else there."

Haiden straightened from the wall and sat on the couch next to her. "You want me to leave?"

He had taken off his hat as soon as her mother pulled him into the house, which left his green eyes clearly visible.

"I don't want you to feel as though you have to be here." She rose off the couch, feeling out of place in her own home.

He stood and pulled her hand, leading her onto the porch, and shut the door behind them.

"I'll leave if you want me to. But I-I want to be here." He squeezed her hand.

"I don't want things to get weird again."

"That won't happen. I had reasons." He took a breath. His eyes focused on her, his fingers threading through hers as he pulled her closer. "I'm sorry about all of that, it was just," he sighed. "I had some stuff going on. I am worried about you, and I want to help."

He pushed some of her hair back, and she flinched, surprised he would do something so personal.

"Okay." She swallowed hard and stepped back. Pulling her hand from his, she pushed them into her pockets. "If you're sure you're okay to stay here, we have a spare bedroom upstairs."

He gazed into her eyes a moment longer, then jumped off the porch to his Jeep.

Haiden Blake was spending the night.

Once back inside, she took her bag upstairs and collapsed on the bed.

"God, what's going on?"

HAIDEN SAT PATIENTLY in the car for Danica and her mother to come out of the grocery store.

Update.

He sighed. Buck only agreed to let him come if Haiden gave him updates.

She's better. Her mother seems in a really good mood too.

I'm waiting for them to come out with groceries.

Let me know if something changes.

Yes, sir.

Why was Buck so protective of Danica? There must be something between Buck, Danica, and Jeff. But he had no idea what.

Seeing her mother be so kind and gentle made him smile. She had been nothing but attentive to him since he showed up, and he had to admit, he found it amazing. Danica had no idea how blessed she had been growing up with a caring family.

Noticing them coming out of the store, he got out of the car to help.

"Who are you?"

He paused as Danica's mother stopped and stared, looking afraid, as she pushed the cart in front of her.

"Mom, remember Haiden?"

"No," her mother scoffed, and he backed away.

"Mom, he's my friend. He brought me home because of the weather."

"Oh? Well then, okay." She rushed past as Danica shook her head and continued to push the cart toward the Jeep.

After unloading the bags in the back, the drive was silent all the way to Danica's home.

"I'll get the groceries." Haiden nodded to Danica. She forced another smile.

He brought in the groceries and stacked them on the counter of the large kitchen. After putting away all the refrigerated items, he turned and saw Danica walking into the kitchen.

"You didn't have to put everything up."

He shrugged as she folded up the paper bags.

"She has dementia. It comes and goes, but I was hoping it would be okay with you here tonight."

He leaned against the counter and watched her flit through the kitchen, shutting cabinets and pushing cans and boxes into place.

"I'm really sorry if—"

"Dani. Don't."

She paused and nodded her head, keeping her back to him as she finished pushing the cabinet doors closed.

"If I need to go, I can go. I don't want to upset her."

"I honestly don't know what to tell you." She started past him, but he grabbed her hand.

She stopped for a moment, finally turning. Her eyes were glassy, and as much as he tried to pull her in, she held fast.

"I just ... I need to check on her."

He nodded and let her go. But that need was back, the one that said he wanted more, needed more, from Danica.

It was something he'd have to forget, to drown out and ignore. Being with him would put her in danger, and he could not let that happen.

18

Danica sat on the edge of her mother's bed, tucking the blankets around her mother.

"You've turned into a wonderful woman, Dani girl." Her mother squeezed her hand. Danica smiled as the light came back into her mother's eyes. It was always there when she was present and not blurry from the Dementia.

"I appreciate that, but I'm not so sure," she said as she stood.

Her mother took her hand and pulled her back down. Danica sat next to her mom, wrapping both her hands around her mother's.

"I know you've had a hard life. Losing your father, almost losing your life, and being afraid for your sister. I know it hasn't been easy."

Wiping her eyes, Danica nodded. "It hasn't, but that's just life. I hate leaving you and Kyra all the time—"

"You're not leaving us. You've got a life outside of us, and that's what's meant to be. God tells us to raise our kids up, let them into the world, and find the path He's laid out for them. Kyra has a path, too, and she'll find it soon enough."

"But I'm needed here."

"I'm fine." Her mother shrugged. "I know I get confused,

and things can be hard." She stared up at Danica. "But God has a path for me, too, and I think I'm on it. I want you and Kyra to be happy, to find a wonderful life with someone you can put your trust in."

Danica swallowed hard and nodded.

"So, tell me, you have a lot of dates?"

"Not really. I ... I have a lot of friends."

"Oh? Tell me about them."

She grinned. It wasn't often she could talk to her real mother and not the shell she found herself with so often.

"Well, I work with Jeff Powers. Do you remember him?"

"How could I forget Jeff? His mother was my best friend. It devastated me when she passed away."

"And then there's Sergio and Evan. A woman named Bexley started working with us, and she's become a great friend. God knew I needed her ..." Her voice trailed off.

"But there's someone else, isn't there?"

She could only shake her head as her mother squeezed her hand. "Haiden. He's a close friend. I ... I just ..." she sighed. "Things have been so off lately. I think he has his own past he's struggling with."

"Do you see in Haiden a future?"

She shrugged, unwilling to voice the thought outright. He had saved her life, been a good friend and teammate. When Danica wanted someone to talk to, his name was the first that popped into her head.

"Finding that one person isn't easy, Dani. Sometimes we've got to forget what we're dealing with in our past and understand that God created us for more than who we once were. And when we live this life, it hurts. But letting others in, it's worth the pain."

Danica nodded, realizing her mother had no idea just how truthful that comment was. Not just with Haiden, but the fact her mother was slowly dwindling away, leaving a shell behind.

"I think I need to go to sleep. It's nighttime, right?"

The light in her mother's eyes was now gone, and she smiled feebly at Danica.

"Yes, Mom, it's nighttime. I'll wake you in the morning."

RUSHING QUIETLY DOWN THE STAIRS, Danica grabbed her coat and went out the back door. Sprinting across the yard, her emotions let loose as she found the treehouse she and Jeff played in as kids. It was only a platform built into a large tree, but she could still find her way up in the dark, balancing on the branches until she reached her spot.

She pulled her legs in and cried. Her heart pounded in her ears. Seeing her mother go in and out, her sister attacked ... It was all too overwhelming.

At the creak of the branch, she jumped up and found Haiden standing next to her.

"What? Why're you here?" She turned and wiped her face as she moved around the platform, placing the large tree trunk between them.

"Dani, stop. Come on."

"Look, I ... I need you to go. I can't ..."

"You're making this too hard, Dani." He took her arms and pulled her into his chest.

Too exhausted to fight or argue, she simply stood there and let him hold her for a moment. His hands rubbed her back, then he sat, pulling her down with him. She pushed away, making some space as she sat and curled her knees to her chest.

"Danica ..." His sigh came through as he scooted closer and wrapped his arm around her. He pulled her in, and her head found his shoulder. "I'm sorry about your mom."

Her body eased into his, hating that he made it all too easy.

"Why are you doing this?" she whispered.

"W-what?"

She groaned and pushed away, crossing her legs between

them. "This. We can't keep going back and forth. I can't handle —do you not see it?"

Poised to speak, he dropped his head. "Danica I ... I don't do w-well... I'm not good at this."

"Good at what? You've always talked to me. I just don't get it. We need to fix this now. Why are you here?"

"I'm concerned about you. I w-want to help."

"Help what? You can be a friend at work. You can be my friend and call or text to check on me like you did yesterday. But here? Why are you here?"

"Dani, I'm trying." His eyes found hers, and she could see him struggling as his breathing increased. He opened his mouth to speak, but nothing came out.

She grabbed his arm. "What's wrong?"

"It's hard to speak sometimes."

She nodded. Leaning against the tree, her body shivered.

"Let's get inside."

Haiden jumped off the side and she stood with a huff. Following his lead, she jumped and smiled as he caught her, holding her steady when she landed. She turned to leave, but he pulled her in close, wrapping his arms around her waist.

"Haiden."

"Just hang on."

She waited. His eyes close a moment, the moonlight giving her just enough light.

He sighed. "I care about you."

"I know." She stopped as his finger pushed on her lips and his eyes focused on hers.

"I need you to know. I just can't do more. I ... I w-want to, but ... I can't."

Searching his face as he held hers, his thumb rubbed across her jaw and pushed her hair back.

She stepped back, pulling from his grip. "What does that mean?"

"Danica, I ... there's so much you don't know."

"Then, tell me."

He shook his head. She pulled completely from his reach and turned to head back to the house, her body shivering from the cold.

Falling onto the couch, she turned on the TV and ignored the sound of the back door opening and closing. She found a movie and pulled the blanket over herself.

Haiden lifted her legs and sat at her feet.

"I ... I have a hard time talking because," he sighed. "I have a stutter."

She frowned. "I've never noticed a stutter."

"Because I don't talk."

"And that's the only reason?"

"Yes."

"Are you sure?"

"Dani."

She sighed. "I've not heard it when you do talk. I've never even thought you had any issues. Even though you seem to side a little too often with Evan and Jeff."

"I side w-with them, huh?"

"Yes, all the time." She nudged his leg as his hand gripped her knee. "Haiden, you better not." Sitting up, she glared.

A smirk formed on his lips.

She kicked out when he squeezed, making her laugh. "Stop it!" she whispered loudly and grabbed his wrist.

A series of hand holds later, between their laughter and their wrestling for control, she leaned her head into the back of the couch. He smiled.

"Haiden, why don't you smile? You have a nice smile."

"I don't smile?" He smirked, and she shook her head.

He pulled at her arm, but she held fast, so he leaned in, and the smile vanished. His green eyes searched hers for a moment, and he released her hand, gently moving his thumb across her cheek.

"Don't," she whispered. Her heart pounded.

"W-why not?" His green eyes looked into hers, and she took a breath.

"You just said you can't."

He sighed, his fingers moving the hair from her face as he rested his head next to hers. "I know, but ... maybe ..."

"I can't do halfway, maybe, or benefits. You need to decide what you want," she whispered.

"I know wh-what I want." His jaw clenched as he leaned close. She could see the brown flecks in his eyes against the dark green iris. "I'm just not sure I can."

"Why not?"

His gaze dropped. He pulled up her hand and kissed it, then leaned back into the couch with a heavy sigh.

She waited, watching his jaw clench and his attractive profile stare straight ahead as if he had a weight on his mind. Curling into a ball, she leaned into his body. She gripped his arm with both of hers, wrapping him up and squeezing.

"I've been dealing with my, my d-dad."

"You two don't get along?"

"No." He blew out. "He w-was a bad guy."

Suddenly, things clicked into place. The way he pushed her behind him at the hospital when his dad showed up, the scars on his back ...

"Haiden, do you think you'll be a bad guy too?" She whispered the words, wondering just how much she should say.

His leg jumped, and she got her answer even if he didn't voice it. Letting him have the silence, she leaned into his shoulder and closed her eyes.

Lord, give Haiden some grace. Let him see who he is in You and that he can be whoever he wants to be. I need him.

The silence filtered through the sound of the TV. His leg finally eased, and his body relaxed into hers.

"You ... you asked me w-what I wanted. What do you want, Dani?" His whispered words made her smile.

"I honestly don't know right now. Things are ..." she sighed.

"Everything seems upside down, and I'm just ... clinging, I guess."

He squeezed her hand. "It'll get better. God has a plan."

She nodded, rubbing her face against his arm and trying to keep her tears from falling. Releasing her hand, he wrapped his arm around her shoulders.

"Don't cry. God really does have a plan," he whispered.

Gripping his neck, she released all her pent-up emotions about her mother, sister, and even the situation with him. This life was hard, and she was so tired of hard.

Her sobs eased, and peace washed over her as Haiden sat there holding on.

19

"I finally got through to Roltz." Buck entered the kitchen and set his tablet on the island next to Jeff. "He requested a meeting this afternoon, if we can fit it into our schedule."

Jeff huffed. "Sure, a last-minute meeting, hoping to catch us at a bad time. Guy is adamant he stay in charge of the situation."

"He wants Dani to come along."

"What?" Jeff leaned into the island as Buck sat back against the counter, sipping his coffee. "Why does he want Dani there?"

Buck shrugged. "Don't know."

"Is she headed back?"

"Yeah. They should be back soon."

Jeff's finger tapped the countertop.

"Problem?"

He shrugged. "No, I guess not. But why does he want her there? We handle the callouts, not her."

"Maybe she said something more than what she let out earlier. Maybe she made a comment he's holding on to."

"You know Dani's not a hold back kinda woman."

Buck sat down his coffee cup. "No, but she was under a lot of stress at the gala. Everything with the office and Bexley. Then this with Haiden."

"About that—why did you let Haiden take her? We're short-handed as it is."

"She needed help."

"I'm just wondering if Haiden's the right man."

"He is."

"Why? Because he's a former Ranger?"

Buck chuckled. "That, and I think he's a good man. I've waited a long time for her to reach out to someone, to trust in someone enough to help her with what she's carrying. She's picked him."

Jeff frowned. "But what if there's stuff in his past you don't know about?"

"I doubt there's anything you know that I don't."

That was probably true.

"I know you're worried. But I wouldn't push anyone who didn't want to be there. Haiden came to me. This was his call, and I just approved it. Besides, this thing with Roltz—it doesn't make sense, and I'd rather someone be with her, just in case."

"In case what?"

Buck shrugged and grabbed his tablet. "Let me know when they get back. I want to get there before mid-afternoon."

Jeff chuckled as Buck headed to his office. Louis Roltz was a shrewd businessman, but he had no idea what Buck was capable of. Buck had been on operations with way scarier and more intimidating men than this guy.

But Roltz had an agenda that centered on Danica. The whole situation didn't sit right with Jeff.

"I'M JUST NOT sure what happened."

Standing at the nurses' station in the nursing home, Haiden observed the conversation between Danica and the nurse who was in charge of her mother.

Danica shrugged. "She mentioned leaving, and someone gave her a ride home."

"The night nurse said a door was left open in one of the hallways. But you have to have a key to unlock it. Otherwise, an alarm will sound. No one has used it for a long time. It's more for emergencies."

"Do you have video?" Haiden crossed his arms.

The nurse's face went red. "No. I mean, not in the hallways. Just in the central areas."

"It's fine, Molly. I know it was an accident. But I don't have anyone who can help, and we're dealing with a situation at work."

Molly took hold of Danica's arm. "Don't worry. I don't need you to give me an excuse. We've known each other too long for that. She'll be safe here for as long as she needs to stay. I'll make sure of that."

Danica sighed. "Yeah. Thanks a bunch." She held up the large envelope. "I'll get the paperwork filled out. As much as I'd like for her to be closer, this place seems to work. I should be back this weekend to visit."

"No problem. Let me know if you need anything else." Molly waved and headed down the hallway.

"Why did you say that?"

He glanced down. Danica had her hand on her hip and a frown on her face.

"What?"

"Asking about cameras?"

"It seemed odd, out of place that a door was left open."

"Accidents happen, Haiden." She pushed past him to the front door. "I'm just glad that someone recognized her and took her home."

He held the door open for her, and they headed to the parking lot. "What did she mean, you've known each other for too long?"

She shrugged. "She and Tony were close for a while. We all

went to school together. They dated some, and I think they're still off and on. She became part of that inner circle we all have in school. The people we can trust."

His jaw clenched as he opened up the Jeep and let her inside. Slamming the door, he headed for his side. An inner circle? He had those friends, the ones who let him crash on a couch, sleep in their garage instead of going home. Those guys had saved his life.

He slid behind the wheel and started the Jeep. "You want to go to the hospital?"

She nodded. "I hope mom will be okay here. I just don't know what else to do right now. I want to wait for Kyra to decide, and I—"

"Dani." He grabbed her hand and squeezed. "You're doing what you can. This is a good place. You and Kyra will figure it out once she wakes up."

She let out a sigh. "Yeah, I know."

At the hospital, Haiden leaned against the wall in the hallway while Danica stood inside Kyra's room and talked with the doctor.

Being around Dani, talking to her about his issues, her issues, getting closer than he imagined—it was surreal. It had taken all his energy to keep from pulling her in and showing her just how much he cared for her last night. But a kiss like that would just prod something more, and the risk was too much to ignore.

"Thanks, I appreciate the update."

Danica stepped into the hallway, a doctor in tow.

"Like I said, everything looks good. We're just waiting for her to wake up on her own. Sometimes that takes time. But we'll call you just as soon as she wakes."

"Thanks."

Danica shook the doctor's hand, then stood staring as the man left.

"Dani?"

Her glassy eyes met his, and he pulled her in for a hug. "I thought the doctor said she was okay?"

"She is." Her voice sounded muffled as she wrapped her arms around his waist. "It's just hard seeing her like that."

He swallowed the lump in his throat and gave her a squeeze before stepping back. She wiped her eyes and kept her face downward, letting out a sigh. He had stepped away again and his stomach churned.

"We should get going. Storms are coming."

She nodded and started down the hallway without him.

"I'll get the car," he mumbled, and rushed out into the parking lot.

The wintery mix of sleet and rain pelted the windshield, and Haiden struggled to breathe as he sat in the car.

"Wh-what are you doing?"

He was falling head over heels for a woman who was way too good for him. If she had any idea where he'd come from, what kind of monster he'd grown up with, she'd run.

Pulling under the portico, he waited as she made her way outside.

In silence, they headed back to Dallas.

"Thanks for coming in. You could've waited outside."

"I wanted to be there." He glanced over.

She was pushed against the door, staring out the window. In one moment, he'd fractured the relationship they were building back. But she just didn't understand.

"Haiden! Look out!"

An SUV from the other lane veered into theirs.

"Hang on!" He shifted to a lower gear and eased the brakes on the slick road.

The Jeep shuddered and slid to the right. The backend of the SUV narrowly missed them. In seconds, he had the Jeep back in the lane. He shifted and sped up to get around the SUV.

"Idiot," he growled.

"I don't think it was their fault," Danica muttered.

She turned around in the seat, then faced the front, her cheeks red.

"What's wrong?"

"I thought I saw a truck."

"Someone you know?"

She shrugged. "I'm not sure. But I saw brake lights when the SUV swerved. Weird."

"It's a bunch of Southerners trying to drive in weather they're not used to. No big deal."

"Yeah, no big deal," she mumbled.

20

"We have a meeting with Roltz." Jeff said as Danica dropped her duffle on the floor in front of the kitchen island.

"What do you mean, *we?*"

Jeff grinned. "Buck said Roltz wants to see all three of us."

"But, why me?"

"I don't know. Guess we'll have to find out."

She let out a groan as Buck came from his office. "Why do I have to go?"

"Is Kyra all right? Your mom?"

Danica nodded. "Mom is back in the nursing home, and Kyra is still out. The doctor said she's doing well. They just want her to wake up on her own."

"Good. Go get changed. We're leaving in ten."

"Come on Dani, maybe he wants another dance."

"Shut up, Jeff." She snatched her bag and headed up the staircase.

Once she changed, she was pulling on her boots when a knock sounded at the door.

"I'm coming! It hasn't been ten minutes yet."

"Dani?"

Haiden? She jumped up and opened the door. "What's wrong?"

"Nothing. I've got some errands to run. Let me know how this meeting goes."

She tilted her head as he nervously shifted from one leg to the next. "What's going on? You sure you're okay?"

He nodded. "Buck said we're on hold for the next day or so. No callouts until he clears the air with Roltz and talks to the commissioner. Call me if you need to talk."

She slowly nodded. His behavior was off.

"Be careful." He gave a wink and descended the staircase.

What was that about?

Danica grabbed her coat from the closet and headed to the garage. She slid into the waiting SUV behind Jeff.

"I still don't know why I'm going." Haiden's comments floated around in her mind.

"This meeting is important, Dani. I talked to the commish, and he wants us to play nice and do what we can to make peace."

"But what are we making peace about?" She leaned forward and glared at Buck. "He's got something personal aimed at us, and we don't know why."

"This meeting is to clear the air and smooth everything out. There's no reason we can't be an ally for him during this election."

She huffed at Jeff's assertion. He was always the peacekeeper.

"Did the nursing home have an idea how your mom escaped?"

"No. Molly said someone reported an open door in one of the wings. But other than that, it doesn't really make sense."

"What else did Molly say?"

"What does that mean?" She leaned forward, glancing at Jeff in the mirror.

Jeff shrugged. "Tony mentioned a few dates with her in the last month. I think he's got some plans."

She chuckled. "Molly didn't mention it. But then again, Tony's name didn't come up."

They pulled up to a large office tower in the middle of downtown Dallas. Once inside, Danica's unease jumped as she paced. The Thanksgiving Gala replayed in her mind. She wasn't overly friendly after Roltz's remarks, but she walked away before she could say anything derogatory.

"Calm down," Jeff mumbled.

"I just don't know why I'm here."

"Roltz finally agreed to a meeting, and you were part of that agreement. Just let me do the talking."

She nodded at Buck with a frown.

"He's ready to see you now." The secretary motioned as she stood and opened the large double doors into Roltz's office.

A large mahogany table sat in the middle of the room. Chairs lined either side.

"He'll be here in just a moment."

The doors slammed shut, and Dani sighed.

"He's really interested in making sure we know who's in charge," Jeff whispered.

"Don't let it shake you. I called Commissioner Stonewell before we left. He said he'd be here for this meeting as well." Buck nodded to both of them.

The door opened and in walked Louis Roltz. Pinstripe suit and a crooked grin. Danica clenched her jaw at the memory of him at the gala last year. His bright yellow tie stood out from his blue collared shirt. Diamond-studded tie tack and cuff links glistened in the bright lights.

"I'm so glad you could attend." Roltz held out his hand, and she reluctantly shook it.

"We appreciate you meeting with us." Buck also shook Roltz's hand.

"Of course. I can understand there might be some misinformation out there. But trust me, I want what's best for this great city. Please, have a seat."

Danica sat next to Buck.

"I was told the commissioner would be joining us."

"I'm afraid he's not able to make it." Roltz sat and leaned back in his chair, gaze focused on Buck. "But I don't see why we can't have a civil conversation without him."

"Absolutely." Buck leaned into the table. "I just wanted to be clear. We're not looking to impede the work the police do."

"Let me say something,." Roltz interrupted Buck. "My campaign is eager to do what the previous administration has refused to accomplish. There needs to be more police, more help to protect the citizens."

"Can you tell me why there seems to be some discord between your campaign and our team?" Jeff voiced.

Roltz shrugged. "I know of no discord."

"You've been cited as saying our team needs better standards, and we're going in ahead of the police to usurp their jobs," Jeff retorted.

"I think that was taken out of context."

"There's not really another way to take that comment," Danica mumbled.

Roltz narrowed his eyes, a crooked smirk forming on his lips. "Don't you want to know why I asked you to attend, Miss Freeman?" Letting the silence speak, Roltz chuckled. "After attending your little gala, I wanted to let you know personally that after this year, your funding will disappear."

"What?" Her jaw twitched.

"It's not just my father who seems intent on throwing his money around. There are several of your backers who insist on finding another way, a less expensive way, to protect their homes and interests."

"Exactly what is the draw here?" Jeff interjected. "Our record proves we're an asset to the community. Anyone else would be thrilled about that fact and would encourage support. Why is the destruction of our team even a consideration?"

Roltz stood, buttoning his blazer. "It's a waste. You take

washed up professionals and trade them off as civil servants. What this town needs are actual professionals who are trained with the best standards and who answer to a higher authority."

"Everything we do is by the book. Our training exceeds what the SWAT teams are required to do." Buck stood. "This is personal, and I want to know why."

Roltz's smile widened. "There's nothing personal about wanting the best for the community, to protect those who need protecting."

"You're speaking to a former Army Ranger with two decades of experience in protecting." Danica shoved her chair back and stood.

"Dani."

Ignoring Buck, she continued, "What you're trying to do is create a personal vendetta against a group that your father supports."

"You know nothing about my father." Roltz stepped closer. "I would tread lightly."

She crossed her arms. "Is that a threat?"

Jeff and Buck were at her back, their presence shadowing.

"I don't threaten anyone, Miss Freeman. But I would watch yourself as you face this city and the dangers it holds. Your team hasn't cleaned up the streets as much as you think." His eyes flicked toward something behind her. "Gentlemen."

21

Trudging up Baylor's steps, Haiden released a deep breath. He no longer had an excuse to ignore his family and the situation that was building. He rode the elevator to the cancer wing and knocked on the door to his father's room.

"Haiden, I'm so glad you came back." His mother motioned him in, forgoing the hug this time.

The bed sat empty.

"He's at therapy. He'll be back soon. Have a seat."

Sitting at the small table in the corner, Haiden focused on the wall in front of him.

"Haiden, I know this is a lot. But you have to know, he's a different man now. He's sober and has apologized constantly for what he's done. He's changed."

He shook his head. Nothing was different to him, not yet. There was always the calm before the storm, the day his father would buy him a present and take him for pizza, and then later that night, beat him senseless.

His mother let out a sigh. "I brought in some coffee. Would you like some?"

He nodded.

As she prepared the paper cups, he did his best to focus on

what God would want him to do. Because being here, seeing his father, was the last thing on his list.

The hair on his neck stood. Jumping up, he turned and saw his father finish pushing through the doorway.

"I ... I didn't mean to startle you." His father paused.

"You didn't." He waited until his father walked around the table and sat across from him before he took his seat.

Leaning back, Haiden crossed his arms, observing the normalcy of his parents sitting together, drinking coffee, talking about the storm headed their way. It was surreal.

"I've got to make a phone call." His mother smiled at him as she stood and headed out the door.

"I didn't think you would come back."

Haiden peered at his father. "Neither did I."

His father wrapped his swollen and calloused hands around the small paper cup. Haiden hated those hands.

"I'm assuming you've healed from your accident?" His father cleared his throat.

"Yes."

"And back to work?"

He nodded.

"What's your girlfriend's name? The one from the hospital. She's beautiful."

"Friend," he mumbled, refusing to discuss Dani with this man.

His father shifted in the chair, taking a heavy breath. "I'm guessing your mother told you."

He nodded.

"Then that's one thing we don't need to discuss. Everything I have is going to her. She already has my will."

Haiden nodded again. His father finished his coffee and set the mug down. His face twisted as his eyes saddened.

"Do you have anything to say, Haiden? Or is this normal? I would think you would have something to say, even if it was to yell at me ..." He paused as his mouth dropped. "Or is this who you are because of me?"

Haiden nodded again, not willing to voice anything more.

His father sat with glassy eyes. "I'm sorry, son. You're not stupid. You stutter because of me. It all began when I started drinking. It's my fault you don't talk. I wish I could take back everything ..." His father's voice died out.

Haiden swallowed hard, unable to speak, while his father wiped tears from his face. The stutter did come from his father. Every time his father was upset, Haiden got nervous, making the stutter more pronounced. That made his father more upset. A domino effect, ending with pain. It didn't take long for Haiden to learn that talking didn't do him any good.

"It ... It's in the past."

His phone buzzed, and he stood, pulling it out and heading for the hallway, thankful for the reprieve.

"Hello?"

"Hey."

His heartbeat spiked at the sound of Danica's voice. "You okay?"

"Yeah, I was actually calling to check on you. *You* okay?"

He smiled. "Better now. Thanks for calling. How was the meeting?"

She huffed. "Terrible. The guy practically threatened me and—"

"He w-what?" Haiden's heartbeat spiked. "Buck didn't say anything?"

"The guy played it off as if it were nothing. He's not going to back down, and now, Buck's about to go full tilt."

Haiden's jaw clenched. "Good."

"Tell me what's going on."

His heart pounded, prodding him on. "I had to check on someone. My ... my d-dad."

"Is he okay?"

"No, not really." Leaning against the wall, he closed his eyes. "He's sick, and I'm not sure what I can do."

"Is his illness bad?"

"Yes."

Her heavy sigh echoed over the line. "Haiden, I don't know what he did or anything, so I can't imagine what you're dealing with. But if he's that sick, you need to pray for help to forgive him for whatever he did. You know you'll regret it if he passes and you haven't made that peace with him."

"I ... I can't." The words caught in his throat. "I know I have to, but ... but I can't."

"I'll be praying for you." She paused a moment. "My mom said something the other day I can't get out of my head. She said we sometimes refuse to forget our past and understand that we're created for something more than who we once were. That living this life, it hurts, and ..."

"And what?"

"Nothing. That wasn't really part of it. But I think the rest definitely applies."

"Yeah, thanks."

"Let me know if you need anything else."

"I will. See you later."

"Bye."

He hung up and leaned his head back against the wall. She had no idea how much those words fit his life. He'd all but moved on from his past, yet it still caught up to him. Control him. He needed to forgive and move on.

"Haiden?" Tony Carlisle gave a nod as he walked up. "I thought that was your Jeep in the parking lot. What're you doing here?"

"I know ... someone," Haiden mumbled.

Tony frowned. "I don't usually work this floor, but they needed help today. Sorry about whoever you're here about."

"Thanks."

"Where's Dani?"

Haiden shrugged. "At the office."

"How's Kyra? And her mom?"

"They're good. We had to go get her mom yesterday and put her back in the nursing home this morning. She somehow escaped."

Tony's jaw clenched as he nodded. "That's not good."

"She's fine now. Kyra is still out."

Tony nodded, his jaw shifting back and forth. "Well, I've got to get to work. It's good to see you out and about."

"Yeah, thanks."

Tony headed down the hallway toward the nurses' station.

Last fall flooded Haiden's mind once more. Tony had been his nurse while he recovered from the blast that destroyed the team's office and embedded shrapnel in his back. Dani had stayed with him for days while he was unconscious. Jeff said she refused to leave.

Her words echoed in his mind.

Forgiveness.

Could he really forgive his father?

22

Danica finished loading the office groceries into her car and slid inside.

It was freezing outside, but they had nothing to eat at work. With Jeff and Buck on the phone tree, trying to find out how their funding fared, and Evan going over tactical training with Bex, they elected her to shop.

Cranking the heat all the way up, she headed from the parking lot, Haiden on her mind.

She leaned back in the heated seat. The last part of her mother's wisdom hung in her throat, and she couldn't even say it out loud. She wanted someone in her life, someone she could trust, and she would gladly risk that pain on Haiden.

But he was unwilling. The fact was more than obvious. Attraction, yes, that wasn't an issue, especially after last night's interactions on the couch. She could've just let him kiss her, and maybe he'd fall just as hard for her.

Flipping the seat warmers off, she sighed. Haiden was one of those guys worth taking a risk on, and right now, amid her trials, she needed more than a risk.

Her Bluetooth rang.

"Hello?"

"Danica Freeman?"

"Yes?"

"Hello. I'm calling from the med center. Kyra just woke up and is asking for you."

Danica's heart pounded. *Thanks, God.*

"That's great. I'll head that way."

"Danica?"

"I'm here."

"Hello?"

Danica checked her phone. It was working on her end.

"Hello? I'm sorry, I can't hear you anymore. I'll try again later."

The call ended.

"Kyra's awake." She whispered a prayer of thanks.

Buck had put a moratorium on callouts, so heading to see Kyra actually sounded much more appealing than whatever training he had in mind. That was a first.

A jolt to her bumper threw her forward, and she let out a yelp as her head slammed into the steering wheel. The rearview mirror displayed a large white truck. Clenching the wheel tighter, she swerved off the highway and onto the ramp, speeding up as the truck gained.

Blood trickled down her face. She swiped it away with the back of her hand. She took a hard right, checked her mirrors, and swerved onto the first road. The truck followed.

"Come on!" She hit the Bluetooth button over and over, but her phone never engaged.

Making a right, she saw the outline of their building in the distance. Speeding through the light, she glanced in her mirror. The truck slowed, finally turning down another road.

"What is going on?"

HAIDEN TOOK a deep breath as he reentered the room, his father still sitting at the table.

"How long?"

It wasn't the question he wanted to ask, but it was the question he needed to ask.

"A few months, years, they don't know."

Haiden frowned. "No treatment?"

His father shrugged. "There are a few, except I'm probably too far gone now."

"You want to die?" He studied his father nervously, rubbing his hands together.

"I don't know about want to. I... I know where I'm going now. But the thought of regrets and the unknown seems, well ... a little scary. Heaven is supposed to be wonderful, you know." He glanced up, his eyes glassy.

Haiden nodded.

"Haiden. I ... I want you to talk to me, even if it's just to yell or scream or whatever. Now that you're here, I just need you to talk."

He paused and sat down, pushing the coffee away. "Mom said you were different w-when ... once you married."

Shock plastered on his father's face. "I was. I ..." the man's shoulders slumped, and he sighed heavily. "You don't remember me back then, do you?"

He shook his head. "Wh-what happened?"

His father wiped his face and nodded. "I let the world win."

Haiden narrowed his eyes and frowned.

"At my job, I had a lot of clients. My boss wanted me to take them out one night. I could do that, no problem. I was good at getting accounts, getting businesses to partner with us. Then, he asked me again later that week. In three weeks, I had become the party guy. If a client needed to be persuaded, I was the guy to help set things up. Suddenly, I was drinking four, five times a week." He shook his head.

"Then other things came into play. Drugs, prostitutes, more

alcohol. I couldn't say no. It wasn't something that just happened." His father groaned and leaned back.

"Within six months, I was different. I had to drink at work just to stay lucid. I drank when I got home, and the person I had been disappeared. I didn't recognize my own reflection."

"Your mother threatened to leave. So, things got violent. I guess I thought I had to make her stay. It was all me, son. I was the bad guy who did this to you and to your mother."

The look on his father's face made Haiden's heart hurt.

The memories came crashing down, and suddenly, none of it mattered as much.

"Why do you ask?"

He shook his head and stood.

"You won't become me. I have no doubts."

"You can't say that. You didn't expect ... this to happen, did you?" He swallowed the demanding tone seeping through his words.

"Haiden."

He turned at his father's quiet voice, a lump forming in his throat. His father patted the tabletop.

"Come, sit down."

He sat, easing back in the chair.

"I was foolish, son. Looking for a name for myself, needing to find my place in this life. I was searching, but I needed God and didn't know it. You've already got the one thing in life you need more than anything.

"You will stumble, you will fall, but I have no doubts you will hear God's voice calling even if you fall into a pit. I created myself into the man I became because I didn't have God with me. I ignored His calls." He stopped and tapped the table in front of him.

"Somehow, God's grace covered you and brought you out of the fire with an amazing character. I see Him inside you, and I know you're a man of integrity. Something I don't think I ever was as an adult." His father's voice wavered and fell as a shaky hand wiped his eyes.

"I will never ask anything of you, son. Even in forgiveness, I know it won't come. But I do ask that you know I am not your future. I've already stolen your past. Don't let my mistakes cost you your future."

Haiden swallowed hard as his father took a ragged breath, his gray, tear-filled eyes staring up at him.

"I ... I think I'll lie down a bit."

Barely able to stand, his father hobbled to the hospital bed. A groan echoed as the bed creaked. The sliding shuffle of rough blankets muffled his movements.

Haiden stood at his father's bedside, observing pain etched on the man's face as his body shivered. He grabbed the blanket at the foot of the bed and draped it over his father.

"You, you should get the treatment."

His father's eyes opened, tears streaming from the corners to his yellow cheeks. "Why would you want me to? I deserve to suffer."

"If you're saved, your debt has already been paid. Don't do this because of ... because of me."

His father gingerly sat up.

"I ... I want to try. Try to forgive you." Haiden worked his eyes across the room, looking for a point to focus on when his father's hand gripped the blanket in front of him, a wedding band still on his finger. "Is that ..." Haiden pointed to it.

His father pulled and rotated the band. "I never took it off. After the divorce, I ... I couldn't."Haiden nodded, staring at the gold band glued to his father's swollen hand.

23

"So, someone hit your car while you were in Hico, and you didn't tell us?"

Danica rolled her eyes at Jeff's tirade. "Ow," she winced.

Buck stepped back, a bloody gauze in his hand. "You're lucky it's just a superficial cut. Otherwise, you'd be going to the ER for a scan."

"I told you, they didn't hit me that time. It was just a bump, and then they sped off. It wasn't a big deal."

"Yes, it is." Buck's jaw clenched. "Was it the same truck both times?"

"No. When I was home, it was a red truck with a chrome brush guard. But this time, it was white. I don't know if it was the same truck that hit Kyra, though."

"Wait, someone hit Kyra on purpose?" Jeff's jaw dropped. "Why didn't you tell me?"

"I just didn't think to tell you." She slid off the top of Buck's desk. "Look, this stays between us."

"It's not like you can hide that cut." Buck shook his head. "Let's put in a police report, just in case."

"In case what? I have no idea who it is."

"I think I do." Jeff handed her his phone. "I found this last night."

He pulled up an article with a picture of Louis Roltz on the front. "New front-runner has big ideas for east Dallas area."

"That article details a new police station and a larger, divided SWAT team that can handle callouts at a faster rate."

"So, he *would* put us out of business. We already know that's what the plan is." She frowned at Jeff. "Why would he want to run me off the road? If he wins, he'll get what he wants. Why would he target me?"

"Look at the pictures at the bottom."

She scrolled down and found a series of pictures of the candidate with his family in front of his home. A large, white pickup truck sat in the background, next to a red truck with a large chrome grill and rims.

"His brother is a car dealer. That article has a link to another that features his car collection."

"There's no way someone like him would use a personal car to attack me."

"After what happened in that meeting yesterday, I think we should be concerned."

"What happened?" Haiden's deep voice echoed in the room. As she turned, his eyes zoned in on her head. "Dani?"

Quickly closing the gap, he brushed her hair from her face, staring at the bandaged cut on her forehead.

"Someone tried to run her off the road," Jeff murmured.

"W-where? Here?"

She nodded and pulled his hand from her face. "I'm fine. I need to go."

"You're *not* fine." Buck spoke through gritted teeth. "If this is related to Kyra—"

"W-wait." Haiden's jaw clenched. "Kyra was run off the road?"

"The police confirmed a white truck slammed into her and pushed her into the tree." Danica's heart pounded at the look on his face. She turned to Buck. "I've got to get to the hospital. Kyra's awake. The nurse called, but my phone cut out, and then the truck came ..."

"Let me see your phone."

She handed it to Jeff. Haiden's hand rested on the small of her back.

"It just shut off?"

"No. I was talking to a nurse, but he said he couldn't hear me. When I was driving back, I couldn't get it to link to the Bluetooth and was too busy trying not to die to fix it."

Jeff frowned and took the phone to Buck's desk.

"I'll take you."

She turned to Haiden. "You need to be here with your dad."

He shook his head. "No. You're not going anywhere alone."

"Haiden."

"He's right."

Groaning at Buck, she headed toward Jeff. "Just give me back my phone so I can get out of here. I don't have time for all of this."

"There's something here," he mumbled as he scrolled through the screen.

"Here. Take a backup." Buck searched through his desk drawer and pulled out another phone, powering it on. "It has all of our contacts. Leave yours here with Jeff so we can figure out what's going on."

"You think Roltz did something to my phone while we were at his office?"

Jeff and Buck pulled theirs out, too, and she moaned.

"Really?"

"If you want to go, go. I'm not risking a callout unless the commissioner himself calls." Buck's eyes jumped behind her. "I expect a phone call if anything goes off."

"Yes, sir." Haiden's militant response rang out as she retreated from the room.

"Let me grab my bag," she called over her shoulders as she rushed upstairs.

Grabbing a bottle of pain medicine, she took a few for her throbbing head. She threw a handful of clean clothes in her duffle, zipped it shut, and headed down the stairs.

JEFF STARED at the Trojan Horse set up on Danica's phone.

"So, what you're saying is, someone had control of her phone?"

He frowned up at Buck. "Maybe not control. I don't think that's what it's for." He pointed to the app discretely hidden in plain sight next to her other apps. "It can monitor calls if the person who put it on there is close enough. It can also monitor where she's going and the phone numbers she's dialing."

"How'd it get there?"

"I don't know," Jeff mumbled. "She could've accidentally downloaded it from an email."

"Dani's too smart for that. We both know that."

Jeff searched his phone for the same app, but it was absent. "It's not on yours?"

"Nope." Buck shoved the phone back into his pocket. "Yours?"

"Nope. Just Dani's."

"How sure are you?"

Jeff stood and punched in a phone number. "I'm about to find out."

24

Danica gently took her sister's hand. Kyra lay asleep and pale, looking like the little girl Danica remembered. Before the chaos that destroyed their lives hit, and Kyra had a future.

"Dani?" Kyra's pretty green eyes opened. "Are you okay?"

Danica nodded. "I'm good. How do you feel?"

Kyra let out a groan. "Like I got hit by a bus."

"It was a truck."

Kyra groaned at the comment. "Not funny."

"Too soon. Got it." Danica winked, and Kyra closed her eyes again. "The doctor told me you're doing well. All you need now is for your leg to heal up."

"Sure, that's all," Kyra muttered.

"I ... I need to ask you a question."

Kyra pulled her hand from Danica's and searched the bed rail. Raising herself up, she slowly opened her eyes. "What's up?"

"I just need to know. No judgment, but ... are you using?"

Kyra's face turned bright red. "What? Are you serious?"

"Kyra, I'm sorry, but I had to ask."

"Why would you think that? I've been clean for four years."

Danica stood and walked to the edge of Kyra's bed. "I just need to know the truth."

"I always tell you." Kyra winced as she leaned forward. "I've always told you what was happening, and I'm telling you now, I'm not using."

Danica sat next to her. "The police think you were run off the road. A white truck rammed you so hard, it wedged you into a tree."

Kyra shook her head. "W-why would someone do that?"

"They think it might be drug related. That you owe someone—"

"I told you. I'm not using." Kyra pulled her sleeves up with shaky hands and held her arms out. "Check me. Do a drug screen. I'm clean."

"Kyra."

"I haven't had any contact with anyone from that life. That's over. I came home one night, and Mom was so confused she did not know who I was. I decided then I couldn't do that to her. I just couldn't keep living that life."

Danica took her sister's arm and lowered it to the bed, covering her up with the blankets. She stared into Kyra's red eyes as tears rushed down her cheeks and nodded.

"I believe you. I'll let Riley know you're awake. They'll want to talk to you, okay? Just tell them the truth."

Kyra nodded, wiping her cheeks with the back of her hand. "Did Tony reach you?"

"Tony? When?"

"He called that day looking for you. I told him to call your phone, but he said it just went to voicemail."

Danica frowned. "I didn't have any missed calls from anyone that day."

Pulling the blanket up under her chin, Kyra shivered. "I know it was him. He asked what I was up to, and I said I was going to a job interview. He knows Jake, the owner of the coffee shop, and said it was a great place to work."

Kyra slid into sleep.

Danica took hold of her sister's hand and let out a breath.

It was wonderful news that Kyra wasn't using. But if she wasn't back into drugs, then who would run her off the road?

AFTER A QUICK VISIT with her mom, Danica leaned back in the seat while Haiden drove her home.

"You don't have to stay."

"Oh? What car are you going to drive?"

She huffed. "My mom's truck is in the garage. I can use it."

"You're not going to stay here alone."

Cutting her gaze to her left, she frowned. "I'm not in any danger here. I mean, if someone is trying to sabotage our team, being here is probably the safest place to be."

The thought almost pushed the air from her lungs.

"If it's Roltz, Buck'll take care of it," he muttered.

Haiden pulled into the drive, and Danica yanked the car door open. She reached for her duffle from the back seat.

"I'll get it." He eased her aside, the smell of his cologne wafting around them. "Let me go in first."

His hand in hers, he pulled her up the steps, and she unlocked the door. He stepped inside and was clearing the rooms when she realized standing in the open doorway was useless.

What was wrong with her? She became completely oblivious when he was around.

Stepping inside, she called out to Haiden. "I'm going to pack up more of Kyra's things to take to the hospital."

Haiden walked into the kitchen, giving her a nod as she eased her way upstairs. Her head was spinning.

Collapsing on her bed, she rolled onto the comforter and closed her eyes. Nothing made sense. She was overjoyed that her sister was clean, but then who would hurt her? Was it to get to Danica instead, and Kyra was an easier target?

She groaned and sat up, finding Haiden leaned against the doorway in her room.

"I thought you were packing."

"I thought you were clearing the house."

He chuckled, and she found a smile. "You should smile more."

"Don't even start," she muttered. Leaning forward on her knees, she let out a breath. "Kyra said she's clean."

"You believe her?"

She nodded. "I can tell when she's lying. Besides, she remembers that day really well. We've talked so much, there's no way I wouldn't have noticed a difference. When she used, she couldn't hold a conversation."

"What does she remember?" Haiden stepped inside and perched on the edge of her desk.

"Tony called asking if she'd seen me. Something about not being able to get a hold of me. But I didn't have a missed call that day, so I think maybe she misunderstood."

"Did she remember the truck?"

"No." Chewing on the inside of her cheek, she shook her head. "It just doesn't make sense. That kind of attack is personal. But Kyra doesn't have enemies."

"You think this is about you?"

Her eyes cut to his for a moment. "Maybe. But then again, if it's me, it's the entire team. I mean, I don't think it's just me being singled out."

He frowned. "On the drive the other day, you mentioned a truck."

"Yeah," she sighed. "The first time I came home, after I heard about Kyra, I was driving through town from the nursing home. A red truck came up behind me, tapped my bumper."

His eyebrow jumped.

"I pulled over, and the truck went by. I think it was just some kid who thought I was someone else."

"And now?"

"Yeah. Now I don't know. When we were driving the other day, I thought I saw a red truck on the other side of that SUV that almost hit us. But I couldn't say for sure."

"If you had told me, I could've kept an eye out."

"It wasn't a big deal then."

He let out a sigh. "Dani, you've got to let other people help you."

"I let people help. Sometimes."

Haiden smirked. "At least you sound like you understand what's going on now. Tell me when something is off. Got it?"

"Yeah, yeah," she mumbled.

"You want to stay the night or head back now?"

Holding her aching head, she let out a sigh. "I don't know. I don't want to make that decision right now."

"How's the head?"

"Not great."

"Lay down and take a nap. It might help if you got some sleep."

"That might be a good idea."

Laying back down, she rolled into the blankets and closed her eyes. A cool blanket fell over her shoulders.

"I'll be downstairs."

A squeeze of her arm, and she was alone, her mind fighting for some peace as she fell asleep.

25

Haiden stared at the pictures hanging in the living room. Danica was beautiful, even when she was a young girl. She had the best smile—big and bright, just like now. He hadn't seen that smile recently.

Sighing, he leaned his head back and closed his eyes. Thoughts of something more than friendship pushed into his mind, and he tried to ignore them. It was much more than an attraction pulling him toward Danica. Although, admittedly, that part was more difficult to ignore the more he was around her.

But she was a missing piece in his life. She made him feel much more than anyone else, and it was creating a current he couldn't get out of. Happiness, love, intimacy, friendship, all those things he'd heard buddies talk about with their significant others that he thought would be impossible.

With a past like his, who would want to take a chance on a man who could so easily fall into the same pitfalls that destroyed his father's life, and in turn, his mom and his own?

The stairs creaked, and Danica came down the steps, wearing a sweatshirt that hung down over her hands, two sizes too big.

"Why aren't you asleep?"

She shrugged and sat down in the recliner, her gaze focused on her phone.

"Dani?"

"I can't ..."

Her tired eyes searched the screen. She was all but asleep when he left the room earlier.

"You need some rest. I know you're not sleeping. I hear you pace at night."

"What?"

"My room is right below yours."

"Oh ..." She fidgeted with her phone.

"Dani? Tell me wh-what's wrong." Kneeling down in front of her, he caught sight of tears falling off her cheek. He pulled her into an embrace. Sobs shook her body. Lifting her, he sat down and held her in his lap. She curled into a ball.

His heart pounded. What could possibly make her this upset?

"If someone did something, tell me—"

"No, it's not like that," she whispered. "Not completely." Wiping her eyes dry, she sat up and sucked in a deep breath. "I ... There was an incident when I was younger. Everything that's been happening lately, it's all compounding, and making those memories come back."

He brushed the hair from her shoulder. "Tell me."

Her pretty amber eyes locked with his. "It's been a long time since I talked about it."

"Then maybe it's time."

She nodded and let out a sigh. "I was almost fifteen and spending my summer at home. "

Shifting from his lap, she settled on the couch next to him. He pulled her hand to his, threading his fingers with hers.

"My sister was following me around and I, I ..."

He squeezed her hand. Teary eyes met his.

"I was outside, walking along the hayfield and picking the seeds off the tips. An abandoned house sat on the other side of the field in the woods. I just wanted to get away from the house."

"Slow down." He wrapped an arm around her shoulder, pulling her in as she took deep breaths.

"I convinced Kyra to go with me. We climbed over the old fence, and I peeked through a window to be sure no one was there. It was empty.—Inside were dirty wooden floors that creaked, and wires hanging from the walls. No boxes or furniture. I guess I was hoping for a treasure hunt or something." She shrugged.

"We started toward the back door when something huffed. I thought maybe a dog was inside. There was this weird smell, like musty old rags covered in cheap cologne, and I just knew someone was there, watching us. I yanked Kyra's arm, and we took off out the back. But a man followed us," she whispered. "Kyra got away, but he ... he shot me."

"Wh-what?"

"There was an empty grave and—and Tony's mom," her voice trembled. "She ... she was lying there. Not sure how long I was there ... until Buck came—"

"Buck? Dani, hang on." He took a few breaths, trying to calm at the thought of her being shot. "Wh-who was this man?"

"Tony's uncle."

"His uncle killed his mom?"

She nodded and pulled her knees to her chest.

"Why?"

"I don't know. I never really ... I mean, Tony never wanted to talk about it, and then his sister tried to commit suicide ..." Her voice trailed off. She closed her eyes as she leaned into the couch.

Wrapping her up again, he pulled her to his lap. "What happened with you, and why was Buck there?"

"He's my uncle," she whispered.

"And what about Jeff?"

"He's like my brother. His mom and mine were best friends.

He was always over. When his mother passed away, Buck kinda took him in. Tony and Jeff and I—we were all pretty close back then."

At least that explained that connection.

"Tell me what happened."

Her head leaned against his shoulder, and she relaxed her legs to the couch. Taking his hand, she held it with both of hers, running her fingers over his knuckles.

"When we ran out the back and into the woods, there were fresh dirt piles. Then I-I recognized her shoes. Those motionless purple shoes pointing to the sky. I told Kyra to run and not stop," she whispered.

"Buck saved me. Stopped the guy from bury ... buying me." She took a deep breath. "I went to the hospital and was in therapy for years. Kyra didn't do so well. The fear overwhelmed her. Even with the therapy, she just couldn't deal. She started drinking. It wasn't long before she was into harder drugs and went into rehab."

"And you?"

She shrugged. "I left. I couldn't be here anymore, be around the house, the field. I can see the woods from my bedroom window, so I chose to leave and forget." Sitting up, her sad eyes found his. "I know it makes me sound like a terrible daughter and sister. But I just couldn't do it, be here."

"It doesn't make you terrible—it makes you a survivor. Most of us have had to make that decision at some point in our life."

Her eyebrow arched. "Even you?"

He nodded. "Even me." Working to ignore her proximity and her fingers tracing his, he cleared his throat. "Um, the man, the uncle—what happened to him?"

"Eugene Barnett, he's in prison. Buck had him down when the police arrived. Poor Tony and his sister had to deal with the fallout. They got a lot of attention, and if I hadn't found him, found the grave ..." She paused and shook her head. "No one would know what happened to their mom and the press wouldn't have pestered them like they did."

"But you helped put a killer away. He could've killed someone else."

She shrugged. "Not sure we'll ever know."

"There's no blame to place, Dani. What happened with Tony's sister is bad, but that doesn't change what his uncle did. He had to pay for his crime."

Letting out a sigh, she stood and paced the living room. "All this mess, trucks ramming us. The unknown. I guess I'm just reliving all the fear I had as a kid. Usually, it eases off. But my typical relaxation methods aren't working. Being here, in this house ... I think it's worse."

He nodded, understanding the need to get rid of past demons. "Have the police found the truck that hit Kyra yet? Or who was driving?"

"Riley's not called me yet about that.."

Knowing she was stressed and not sleeping differed from knowing just how badly she was dealing with her past. And shot? Someone shot her when she was fifteen? What a horrible experience to replay over and over again.

As she paced, her right hand rubbed her left shoulder.

"Is that where?"

She paused, staring a moment, before dropping her hand. "Yeah," she mumbled.

Standing, he pulled her in for a hug. "I'm sorry, Dani."

Her arms wove around his neck.

"I'll keep you safe. You don't have to worry about anything. I'm here."

She nodded and buried her face in his neck. Goosebumps pricked his skin. Letting out a breath, he pulled her hand down and led her to the kitchen.

"What're you doing?"

He opened up the cabinet. "Don't think I missed those

graham crackers and marshmallows from the store." He grinned as she chuckled.

"You never know when you might need some s'mores." She grinned.

Handing her the bag, he opened up the back door, and they stepped into the cool air.

"Let me get my jacket."

She disappeared back into the house as he set down the supplies and started cleaning out the firepit.

Danica reappeared with her coat and a lighter. She pushed around the kindling, and he reached for the lighter.

"I know what I'm doing. A Ranger taught me how to build a fire."

"You have a Ranger here. Let me do it."

She narrowed her eyes and handed him the lighter. "You know, I think the only reason Buck let you drive me is because you're one of his own."

He chuckled as she let out a grin.

The fire roared to life, and Danica pulled down the two metal chairs from the porch. They sat in silence, roasting the marshmallows. As he poked his stick into the embers, his father's words rumbled around in his mind.

"My ... my mom said my dad w-wasn't always like ... like I knew him."

"Do you believe her?"

He nodded. "He's been staying w-with her for a while now. I had no idea what was going on. She called and said to meet her at the hospital. I didn't know."

"How long has he been sick?"

"Several years, I think. He ... he said he found out and then ... God decided he was w-worth saving."

"Do you believe he's saved?"

He nodded. "He has to be. There's no storm."

"Storm?" She leaned in as he nodded.

Scooting her chair closer, her arm linked with his.

"I could see it in his eyes. Even the days things were good. It w-was there."

The light of the flames danced in her wide eyes, the cool, wintery air blowing the strands of hair around her face. He brushed them aside, leaning closer, and ran a finger down her jaw.

The past came to life again along with the overwhelming fear of becoming that man, the one who would hurt Danica's heart, swallowed him.

Leaning back, he cleared his throat. "It's going to rain. We need to get inside." He let go of her hand and stood, breaking the stick and tossing it into the fire.

26

As Danica put everything away in the kitchen, rain pounded on the roof. She wished they were still at the firepit, willing to finish whatever Haiden was about to start before he got up and left. Again.

Haiden was leaning against the counter with a mug of coffee.

"How did you know it was going to rain?"

He shrugged and took a sip, but she could see the smirk from behind the mug.

"Did you watch the weather?"

He shook his head.

She narrowed her eyes. "Then tell me." Danica leaned against the opposite counter, arms crossed as she fixed a glare on him.

Setting down his mug, he stepped in front of her and shoved his hands into his pockets. "I bet Buck did that, huh?"

She narrowed her eyes. "Sometimes."

"Rain and humidity change the air pressure. So, when you shoot, it can change the dynamics of the bullet. After being outside and training for years, it's something you look for." He leaned a hip next to her, then pulled some hair from her face and tucked it behind her ear.

"Something on your mind?"

Her face heated, and she shrugged. He pulled her into his chest, and she rested against him. It was getting easier and easier to just let him in.

"I hope y-you understand," he murmured.

"I guess I don't. Not really."

His heavy sigh lifted her cheek. "Dani, I can't put you in danger."

She eased back to see the worry etched on his face. "Danger? You really think that's what would happen?"

"I can't know." He shook his head. "I can't risk you getting hurt."

Pulling from his grip, everything finally clicked. "You say you can't do more, but you want to, and now you say it's because you might end up ... what? Hurting me? Haiden, you're not your father."

His jaw jumped. "I'm not now, but—"

"No. No buts." Grasping his fisted hands, she forced her fingers through. "You're an amazing man who would do anything for anyone. You're kind and have this big heart. If you think for a second that you would fall under the same devastation as your father did, you won't."

"Dani."

"I won't let you." She dropped his hands. "Don't you think I'd be the kind of woman who would walk away from any man who hurt me?"

A sudden crash sounded and Haiden had her covered on the ground, his elbows propping him up.

"You okay?"

She nodded. Haiden rolled off and sprinted to the back of the house.

The smell of smoke and ash filled the air.

Haiden reappeared. "Call the fire department." He grabbed the fire extinguisher from the kitchen and ran back outside.

Sitting against the counter, she pulled out her phone and called 911.

"Nine one one, what's your emergency?"

"There's a fire behind my house."

"Address?"

"3410 Harvest Road."

"Fire trucks are already in route. Do you need medical help?"

"No, thanks."

Danica stepped onto the porch, holding her sleeve to her face. Haiden was putting out the embers closest to the house. The trees in the yard were ablaze, and a large tree limb had fallen through the dining-room window. Shattered glass was strewn everywhere.

She gasped. "Oh, no." Flames engulfed her treehouse.

"Dani?"

She blinked away the tears and turned to Haiden. "What ... how did this happen?"

"THE HOUSE?"

Danica sighed as Buck's questions continued to pour from her phone. "I told you. The fire didn't get to the house. I'm just glad Mom wasn't here."

"You need to get back here where we can monitor you."

"I'm fine. Really."

Buck huffed. "Dani, between being attacked on the road, and now this? You're going to stay here under lock and key."

She groaned.

"I expect you to be on the road ASAP."

"Yes, sir." She disconnected the call and collapsed into a chair.

DANICA PACED THE LIVING ROOM, waiting for Riley to finish speaking with the fire chief.

Riley stepped into the living room, taking off his hat and running his fingers through his gray hair.

She shoved her hands in her pockets. "Did you talk to him? What'd he say?"

"I've got the initial report down, but this is probably arson. With no lightning reported and the ground wet, nothing goes up in flames like that without help. The yard is badly damaged."

"I figured. Did you hear anything else about Kyra's accident?"

"We're still sifting through it all, but it's going to take some time. We're working as hard as we can, but this isn't the city. I'll let you know if we find out something about her accident and about this incident. You going back to the city?" Riley asked.

"Yes, Buck's eager for me to be under his roof."

"I bet he is. Be careful, Dani. And don't worry—I've got an officer setting up outside Kyra's room for now. Just in case."

She swallowed the lump in her throat and nodded as Riley left.

"Wh-what's wrong?" Haiden sat next to her.

"Riley said he's putting an officer outside Kyra's hospital room," she whispered.

"That's smart. Can't be too careful."

Tears filled her eyes. Once more, it was her fault Kyra was in danger. "Whoever wants my attention is also focused on Kyra. She'd be better off if she moved away for a while."

Haiden placed his arm around her shoulder and pulled her in. "Don't do that. This is on whoever it is, not you. They're the bad guys here."

A kiss landed on the top of her head.

"I'm sorry about your treehouse."

She shrugged. "It's just a thing." Scanning the room, the empty house felt like a shell without her mother and sister around. "Just like this place. I don't think I can keep it."

"What about Kyra?"

"She wouldn't want it. She's talked about selling it several times, and I told her I'd back whatever she wanted to do. But now, I think I'm going to have to make the decision. Mom can't be here alone. Kyra will be in rehab for a while, and I can't move back here." A shudder racked her body.

Looking over her shoulder, she noticed the black smudges of soot on Haiden's face from trying to put out the flames.

He'd risked his life for hers. Again. And all she could do was sit here and stare.

"Dani?" His whispered words drew her closer. He edged his fingers around her jaw.

A loud bang sounded, and her eyes jumped from Haiden to the door.

"Wait here." Haiden headed to the door, holding the handle of his Walther PPK. "It's Tony"

"What?" She stood and grabbed the door handle. Tony stood on the porch, red-faced.

"What's wrong?" she asked.

"What do you mean, what's wrong?" He pushed inside, pausing to stare at Haiden. "What're *you* doing here?"

Haiden crossed his arms.

"He drove me home." She pulled on Tony's arm. "Why're you in Hico?"

Tony's jaw clenched, his brown eyes found hers. "I was at the facility and heard about the fire. You need to be somewhere safe. Let me take you to Buck."

"She's got a ride," Haiden gritted out.

"Dani?"

She frowned. "Tony, calm down."

"Why did you come home? I thought you were keeping a low profile."

"I came to see Kyra and my mom."

"Why didn't you go back to Dallas after that?"

Haiden eased up behind her. His hand trailed along her lower back.

"Tony." Finally getting his attention, Danica pulled his elbow and led him to the couch. "Did something happen to your sister? Is she okay?"

"She's fine. I just ... I was just worried about you." His eyes cut from her to Haiden. "I think you should leave before you get hurt."

"We are. I'm loading my stuff, and then we're headed back."

Tony's eyes shifted. "I think that's a good idea. I ... I'll see you later." With that, he left as quickly as he came.

The slam of the door made her jump.

"What was that about?"

"I don't know." She shrugged and held her aching head. The fumes from the fire were building up inside the house. "I'll go pack and then we can put something over the window."

"You go pack. I'll take care of the window." Haiden turned and left just as abruptly as Tony had.

27

O nce in the car, Haiden sat stone faced, working his mind around what had happened.

After patching the window and loading her bags, he'd been trying to put the puzzle pieces together. Why did Tony show up? The look on his face was too familiar to Haiden. Setting the words in his mind, he took a deep breath.

"W-we need to talk."

"Look, I'm sorry about Tony. I—"

"No, wait." He grabbed her hand. "I need you to understand ... I know w-what I'm talking about."

"Okay."

"I think you should stay away from h-him."

"Tony?"

He nodded. "Look, I'm not ... I'm not trying to tell you w-what to do, Danica. But he's—"

Danica squeezed his hand. "I see something in him. He's dangerous."

"I've known Tony forever. He's just rattled with all the accidents. His sister's in a facility here in town because she attempted suicide. She had some mental issues before..." Danica let out a sigh. "Ever since all that happened, Tony just loses it when things go wrong. He's not a bad guy. He just wants to keep us safe."

Haiden took a deep breath. "Okay. But I want you to understand that there's s-something off." He squeezed her hand. "I don't want you to get hurt."

"Thanks."

His heart still pounded. He pulled his hand from hers and placed it on the wheel. With the continued attacks, he needed to be much more vigilant.

The attacker just escalated from bumper taps to house fires —a bad sign.

"So, here's what my buddy said." Jeff sat at the table next to Danica, her phone in hand. "This app, it's a Trojan Horse. Someone is monitoring you."

"Monitoring me? Are you serious?" She snatched it from his hand and scanned the device. "I never upload anything I don't recognize. How did it get on my phone without me knowing?"

"That's what I thought. I've gone through the system trying to find where it originated from, but no luck."

Shaking her head, she sat the phone face down. "I have no idea."

"Dani?"

She sighed and leaned her head in her hands. "This has been a hard day," she mumbled.

"I'm sorry." He frowned at the bruising around the cut on her forehead. "Let's see if Buck's got traffic camera footage from where you were hit."

"How can he possibly know where I was hit?"

Jeff shrugged. "He knows where you were coming from, and I'm sure he can spot your car. It's not that hard." His phone vibrated, and he pulled it free. "Powers."

"Sutton. You said Danica Freeman would be back in town today. Is she available?"

"Yes, she just got back. I'll bring her in."

"Thanks."

He hung up and stood.

"Bring me in?"

"The police want your statement about the other day. You were one of the first inside. I'm driving."

With a huff, she stood and left her phone as they headed to the garage.

28

The rest of the afternoon was spent at the police station, going over the investigation into the two injured police officers.

"You sure you don't want to file a report? That knot looks pretty bad."

Jeff glared at Sutton, pulling Danica away. "She's good. Thanks for the offer."

"Let me know if you change your mind. Road rage is dangerous, and we don't want anything bad to happen." Sutton called as they headed to the SUV.

"Guy's a jerk," she mumbled, sliding into the seat. "First, he practically accuses us of letting those police officers get hurt, then wants to help me out with the guy that hit my bumper."

He let out a chuckle and headed to the other side. Cranking up the heat, he put the car in gear and started for the office.

"I can't believe you think I have to be driven."

"Buck wanted to have a talk about what happened at the house. You sure you're okay?"

She exhaled. "I'm not okay. I haven't been okay since Kyra was hit." Her glare cut into him. "What else do you want to know?"

"Is Kyra using again?"

"She swears she's not."

"What does Riley say?"

"He just told me he talked to her. I think they ran a drug test to see what was in her system. But I believe her. She has a tell when she's high, and it wasn't there."

"Then who else would attack Kyra?" Jeff kept his eyes on the road, feeling her glare intensify. "Roltz? You really think he's attacking your family?"

She shrugged. "No idea. But I am being singled out. That's the only thing I can think of. But why?" She chewed on the inside of her cheek.

"How's Haiden?"

He chuckled as a pink rush warmed her cheeks.

"He's got his own issues. Something about his dad."

Jeff frowned. "His dad, huh?"

"Yeah."

If Haiden was opening up that much, if that thing with his dad was that bad, maybe he had a good reason for not stepping up.

"He mentioned y'all saw Tony. Where?"

"He showed up after the police left. Said he was visiting his sister and heard about the fire. By the time he showed, he was really worked up. You know how paranoid he gets."

Jeff nodded. Tony had become obsessive of his sister and her safety, and that extended to Danica as well as himself.

Jeff tapped his finger on the steering wheel and eased the accelerator as the light turned green. A revving engine to the left caught his attention.

"What?"

Before the word left his mouth, a truck sped up through the red light, aimed right at him.

"Hang on!"

Slamming the accelerator to the floor, he drove forward, then cut the wheel to the left, fishtailing out of harm's way. The truck sped up and away through the light before Jeff could catch a glimpse.

"Did you get a plate?" He glanced at Danica, who shook her head.

"It was a red truck, right? Was that for you or me?"

"Or us?" he asked. Yanking out his phone, he called Buck. "We've got a problem."

"I KNOW A GUY. I'll get video," Buck said as Jeff collapsed into the oversized chair.

After calling in the possible hit and run, Jeff and Danica waited at the scene and repeated the entire ordeal several times before they could leave.

"I'm guessing you aren't going through Sutton to get that."

Buck peered over his phone.

"Still don't trust him?"

Buck shrugged. "It's not that I don't trust him. I just can't place him. Yet, the way he talks, there's something familiar. Either way, until we figure out who is targeting my people, everything stays in house."

Jeff nodded, turning his phone end over end on his knee. "What if this is about you?"

Buck's gaze shot up. "What?"

"Well, first Kyra, then Danica, now Danica and me. We all connect to you."

"Not everyone leads to Buck," Haiden said, entering the office and sitting next to Jeff.

"Oh? What do you know?"

Haiden frowned. "We avoided a collision on the highway the first time I drove Danica to Hico and back. I just assumed it was bad driving, but she thought she saw a truck slamming on its brakes and forcing another car into us."

"That's still Dani," Jeff sat up in the chair. "Just what did Danica tell you while you were on your trip?"

"Enough."

Jeff's jaw clenched.

Buck nodded. "Good. Now you understand what she's been dealing with."

"It explains a lot." Haiden glanced at Jeff. "A whole lot."

Jeff shrugged and stood. "I'm out. Let me know when you find something on that video."

"Will do," Buck said as Jeff shut the office door.

Checking the house's doorknobs, Jeff let out a yawn. It wasn't even ten, and he was exhausted and confused. The profiler in him screamed this wasn't over and to be prepared. With the fire and the road attacks, the perpetrator was escalating in his attempts.

But what was he attempting to do?

If he really wanted to hurt Danica, he could've set that fire at night—and to the house, not the yard. And the road attacks could've been much worse.

He shook his head and stepped into his room, ready for sleep. If he was right, he would need his rest for what was to come. This fight was personal.

29

"Cold?"

Danica snugged her blanket tighter around her shoulders and stared at Bexley bustling around the kitchen. "What do you think?" She sat on the barstool. "Are you ... cooking?"

Bexley scoffed. "Don't sound so surprised. I found I'm adept at making pancakes. I've also got muffins in the oven."

"A sweet breakfast. My favorite." Danica smothered a yawn.

"Mornin'." Haiden's voice floated from behind her. His hand brushed her back as he sat next to her. "You get some sleep?"

She shrugged. "A little." Glancing up at his frown, she rolled her eyes. "I'm good." She dropped the blanket to the stool and headed to the coffeepot.

"Listen up." Buck walked into the kitchen and looked around. "Where are Evan and Jeff?"

"They said something about the shooting range this morning," Bexley answered.

"I'll fill them in later, then." Buck pulled out his phone and sent a text. "I got the traffic camera footage."

"What? How on earth did you manage that?" Danica stared

at Buck. "Tell me you went through the proper channels." She sat on her barstool and placed her mug on the island.

"Of course. I just have faster friends than the police do." He grinned.

Danica's stool was pulled close to Haiden, and his hand rested firmly on the small of her back, his gaze never leaving Buck. She glanced up at Bexley, who had a huge grin on her face.

"Look at this." Buck held the tablet down for her to see.

A red truck sat at the intersection, halfway inside a parking space, but not blocking traffic. In seconds, the light changed, and the truck roared to life, pulling out and narrowly missing their SUV.

"That was too close," Haiden's drawl sounded.

Her heart pounded at the sight. "You have no idea."

Haiden's arm wrapped around her waist.

"I can't get a read on the plates. My friend's looking at cameras from these shops." He pointed at the screen. "I've been trying to find your hit from the other day to match the truck. Between the shops and the other footage, I have a feeling we'll get lucky."

"I hope so." Jeff entered from the back door, dropping his gear in the living room instead of inside the equipment room. "I just got a call from a buddy of mine."

"You're not gonna believe this," Evan said as he walked in and wrapped Bexley in a hug.

"The officers woke up last night, and they had a lot to say. The stories match up. Basically, as they pulled in front of the business, no one was around, so they went to the back. Once they parked, an automatic rifle pounded their car. One officer said he tried to radio for backup, but it was like they were being jammed. He couldn't get his phone to work either."

"Jammed?" Haiden's voice sounded from behind her.

"That sounds familiar," she mumbled. "So, your buddies just told you all this?"

"They said we've been blacklisted. Buck should get a call

from the commissioner soon with an apology." Jeff crossed his arms. "Anyway, once the shooting stopped, a can of tear gas was tossed into the car, and they were attacked. Both took a hit to the head, and neither remembers anything else."

"Someone set them up to be captured without injury. If you wanted to hit the person in the car, you shoot the windows." Haiden's low voice echoed from behind her.

Buck motioned to his phone and left the room.

"The question is, why? Why lure the police, but not injure them? Did the thieves end up taking anything from the building?"

Jeff shrugged at Bexley's question. "No idea. But thankfully, the police no longer blame us for what happened. Maybe now we'll get some answers. They're going to want to find these guys before they attack again."

"Actually, I think the question is, were they waiting for the rest of the police, or for us?"

She turned to Haiden, who leveled his gaze at her. "You think this is about us?"

"Why not? You've been attacked. Jeff and I have also been in the middle."

"But those men left once the police sirens sounded. Maybe they just wanted to discredit the police?" Bexley frowned. "Also, how does that factor in Kyra's attack?"

"It's a separate incident." Jeff leaned against the island. "That makes the most sense. Kyra's attack is just a coincidence that occurred at the same time as all this. How hard would it be to hire out some men to set all this up?"

"Not hard if you know the right people," Evan answered. "That building is easy to get in and out of—only a few lights between the location and the interstate. They have full sight in front and back. And they placed that truck where no one would notice—in a field that was overgrown as if it was supposed to be there. Frequency jammers are easy to download, and if you know the right people, you can learn what frequency the police are using."

"This is crazy," Danica mumbled. "It makes no sense."

Buck walked in, his face red.

"That doesn't look good." Jeff turned with a frown. "I guess you didn't get an apology?"

"Not in so many words. The commissioner is still getting information. So far, looking at two perpetrators. Nothing was taken from the buildings, but it appears as though someone rifled through them. Maybe they didn't want to resort to killing anyone when the police showed up."

"That's thin." Jeff started pacing. "Who brings an automatic rifle and doesn't plan on using it?"

"Either way, it's not our job to figure it out. We just need to be ready to go. I've put us back on the call list should something come up in our location."

"What about all the attacks?"

Buck shrugged. "We're going to be vigilant and not go out alone. Everyone pairs up."

"You want to go lie down?" Haiden's breath on her neck made Danica shiver under the blanket. "I'm fine."

He frowned. "We talked about getting rest. I know you're not, remember?"

As Jeff and Buck left, Bexley pulled Evan from the kitchen.

"I don't want to lie down. I won't sleep."

"Come on." Haiden stood and pulled the blanket up, taking hold of her hand.

Guiding her to the couch, he sat down and pulled her next to him.

"I won't go to sleep."

"Fine. Just rest." He wrapped the blanket over her, then pulled her close.

Too tired and cold to argue, she curled up at his side.

"I'll save you a muffin," Bexley called from the kitchen.

"Thanks." Danica closed her eyes.

Warmth radiated from Haiden, and she smiled at the woodsy cologne, the way he held her close, his fingers playing with the ends of her hair ... Her mind eased, and she faded into sleep.

JEFF WENT over the video Buck had magically procured.

"Thanks."

He glanced up and saw Buck set down his phone. "Good news?"

"Not about that. I heard from the last donor. Everything looks good, Roltz was playing us." Buck sat at the desk, leaning back in his chair. "Do you think he's got something else at play here? What does he have to gain if he puts us out of business?"

Jeff shrugged. "No idea. I know he's a control freak, and he's got money. He thinks backing this idea of more police and less us will get him elected."

"What bothers me is that Commissioner Stonewell hasn't stepped up for us. I've had conversations with him about all of this. I don't understand why suddenly we're no longer welcome. Our response times are even better than they were last year."

"Then maybe it's the commissioner who has changed."

Buck's gray eyes met his. "Didn't think about that. Maybe I need to do some digging."

"On the commissioner? You think that's a good idea?"

Buck's jaw tensed. "Three years ago, I set this team up with the help of the commissioner and the mayor. They gave me the idea. They pushed for this group to come about. Why would it suddenly not be a good idea? We haven't changed, but one of them has."

Jeff leaned in. "You're not going to go digging on the mayor. You get caught, there goes the only person on our side."

"If he gets re-elected this year."

"Doesn't matter."

"You know I don't get caught." Buck grinned.

Leaning back in the chair, Jeff shook his head. "I may not have the money to bail you out. You're a flight risk, and the judge might not even let you get out on bail."

Buck chuckled. "I've got pull. I'll be fine."

"I guess I'll take your word for it." Jeff's phone vibrated. "Powers."

"Your team ready to go?" Sutton's voice echoed over the line.

"Sure. What's up and where?" He stood and headed for the equipment room.

"We've got a protest going on and need some extra manpower."

"A protest?"

"You've been requested. I'll send you the address."

The call ended, and Jeff snatched his rifle from the locker.

"We're going to a protest?"

He nodded at Evan. "He said we were requested."

"Let's load up. We work this like any other callout."

"I'll tell Haiden. I think Danica is asleep."

"They stay here."

Bexley nodded and rushed from the room.

Jeff headed to the garage and slid into the SUV. He pulled out his phone and set the address in the GPS. "Let's roll."

30

H aiden leaned his cheek against Danica's head.

She'd passed out quicker than he expected. His heart pounded, his mind jumping to all the times he walked away, turned away from her in an effort to not be here. He'd given up all this time with her when it was what he wanted.

His father had mentioned having a future. Nothing in this world could be more important than protecting Danica and being here for her. Whoever was coming after her would have to go through him first, and they wouldn't make it.

She jumped, and her hand flew out as she sat up.

"Dani?"

She turned, wide-eyed and breathing hard.

"You're okay. Lie back down."

Blinking a few times, she gazed around and let out a breath. "Sorry," she whispered.

Pulling her shoulder in, he wrapped her up in a hug. "Nothing to apologize for."

Her body shook.

"Tell me about it."

"What?"

"Your dream. Tell me what happened."

She sighed and sat up, wiping her cheeks. "Talking about dreams never makes them go away. Time is the only thing that has helped."

"Then tell me so I can know."

Holding her chin in her hand, she looked up with glassy eyes. "Dirt. I smell fresh dirt and hear this digging sound."

His jaw clenched.

"I remember thinking I had to keep still, keep my eyes closed. I guess I thought it would help if I didn't see it." Her eyes dropped from his. "I didn't want to see it."

"I remember that ... closing my eyes," he murmured.

She glanced up, her eyebrows furrowed.

"It did help, but it didn't make it go away."

She took hold of his hand. "You want to talk about it?"

He shook his head. "Been a long time ago. It doesn't hit me now."

"Really?" Her tone conveyed her disbelief. "Because even if it doesn't hit you, you've let it affect you. You do see that, don't you?"

"I do. But I'm working on it."

Her eyebrow quirked as her bright lips parted.

"I'll let you know how it goes." He pulled on her hand. "Lean back and get some rest."

"I'll see if I can find that muffin Bexley promised me." She stood and pulled away, ambling into the empty kitchen.

That wasn't exactly the response he expected or hoped for. After pushing her away for so long, she was done waiting on him. The thought shot a pain through his chest. As much as he was accustomed to pain in life, this hurt more than anything else he'd experienced.

Leaning on his knees, he ran his fingers back and forth through his hair, trying to find some courage to go talk to her, tell her how much he cared for her and wanted to be better for her. The sudden fear she wouldn't be interested in risking it stabbed his heart.

Lord, what do I do now?

JEFF SLID from the SUV as a police cruiser arrived next to him.

"At least they made it this time," he muttered.

They had parked a block away from the protest, and Sutton climbed out of his cruiser, a bullhorn in his hand.

"You got a plan for this?"

Sutton shrugged at Buck. "As long as they're peaceful, we've got no issues."

"Just out of curiosity, why call us out? It doesn't look like you need us."

"I got the order from the commissioner." Sutton motioned for them to follow. "He said you guys needed to be included, so here we are." He scanned the area and frowned. "You're missing a few."

"We are." Buck held his hands on his hips, obviously irritated at the callout. "And I will talk to Commissioner Stonewell about this. We appreciate the invite, but we're not riot police."

"Noted," Sutton mumbled.

A gunshot echoed, and Jeff took off with Buck at his heels. As Jeff and Buck turned a corner, a group dressed in red stood in the middle of the road—no signs, no one injured or running scared.

"What's this?" Buck asked.

"I don't know."

Another retort echoed from the tall buildings, and Jeff turned to Sutton.

"I've got my guys going along the outside looking for the shooter. No one appears injured."

"It's a fake." Evan stepped forward, staring at the protesters. "It doesn't sound right. And if it were a gun, those people would be running."

As Jeff approached the crowd, a woman turned and placed her hands on her hips.

"What do you want?" she sneered.

"Why are you here, and what's the point of this riot?"

"Riot? What riot?" The woman in the red dress glared. "I'm here for a political protest, not a riot. That's what the post was for."

Jeff frowned. "What post? And who has a gun?"

"A gun? I don't have a gun." The woman's jaw dropped. "Is this safe?"

He sighed and motioned to the sidewalk. "Can we talk over there?"

She followed as the crowd in red dissipated.

"What post are you referring to?"

She pulled off the bright red hat she wore and took off her sunglasses. "I answered a post on social media about a flash mob here at five after ten." Her fingers flew across the screen of her phone, and she held it out for him to see.

"Come, show your support ... five o'clock ..." he scanned the article. "Don't be late, this is a Total Request Team effort." He glanced up at Buck. "Call Haiden. Now!"

31

"I spoke to my d-dad the other day." Haiden said.

Danica leaned against the kitchen counter, holding her chocolate muffin. "How did that go?"

He shrugged and sat at the island. "I guess okay."

Setting down the muffin, she wiped her hands on the dishtowel and leaned into the island. "How sick?"

"Cancer. He's got liver cancer." Haiden hesitated. "H-he's put off treatment, so ... not sure how long."

She took hold of his hand. "Sorry. That sounds bad."

"I think h-he might get treatment. I don't know if it's too late." His phone buzzed, and then Danica's went off.

"That's weird," she muttered.

Standing, he glanced down the hallway, then to the front door.

"It's Bexley. She said get safe?" Danica's wide eyes met his, and he reached around the island, grabbing her arm.

"Let's go."

"She's trying to explain—"

"Not important." He motioned for the equipment room. "It's a concrete safe room. They can't breech without some pretty heavy equipment. If Bex is calling, then they're on their way back."

He secured the room with an iron bolt then turned to Danica. She stood sheet white, gripping the phone to her chest. "Dani?"

"I ... I don't do so well in small spaces," she whispered.

Double checking the door, he stepped up and took the phone from her hand.

"It stopped working. I lost signal."

"It's a concrete room. You're not going to get a good signal in here." Wrapping his arms around her, he frowned as she trembled. "Hey, we're going to be fine. They're on their way back, and will knock on that door soon to tell us it's safe to come out."

"Why ... why is someone coming here?"

A sudden thud vibrated the room, and Danica let out a yelp.

"Let's sit down." He pulled her to the back corner.

He sat her in the office chair, then pulled his rifle from his locker, shoving his Walther PPK in his waistband.

"I thought you said no one can get in?"

"Never can be too safe." He glanced up at her with a wink. "Learned that in the Army."

"You don't talk about it much."

He shrugged and walked back to her, going down to a knee and setting his rifle on the floor. "Not much I can talk about. Kind of protected information, not allowed to share."

"What made you decide to go in?"

Shouts and sounds of gunfire made her jump.

He took hold of her hand, squeezing until she focused back on him. "I didn't really have a choice. My d-dad wasn't good." He narrowed his eyes, trying to find the words.

"I don't mind, Haiden."

"Mind?"

"I don't notice it. I know you do, but I don't."

He swallowed hard and nodded. "Yeah ..."

"Is it all the time?" Her voice shook.

"No, just high stress, high emotion. It can be h-hard to control. Just certain words." He licked his lips. "I didn't really have a choice but to go into the service. I couldn't get into college, didn't want to."

A knock sounded and Danica tensed.

"Just wait."

Another series of knocks and he stood. "That's Evan. It's safe."

"How, how do you know?"

He helped her to stand, her body in full tremor. "It's a military thing. We can communicate through walls."

"Funny," she muttered, and he chuckled.

He disengaged the bolt and foot lock. Evan stood outside the door, red-faced.

"How bad?" Haiden asked.

"Only a few were here by the time we arrived, and they took off before we could get out of the car." Evan's gaze cut to Danica as the door opened. "They put dummy bombs on the doors and set them off."

"Dummy bombs?"

"All show and sound, no damage," Haiden said, wrapping an arm around Danica.

"This was all to scare us?" Danica searched his eyes.

"I don't know."

"Buck and Jeff are on it. They've got a lot of video from our cameras. We'll get a name this time."

"Come on." Haiden helped her out of the room and to the end of the hallway.

"I'm good." She stepped back, holding his arm. "Sorry about that. I don't normally freak out. It's just all of this, and we talked about my ... my dreams."

"Stop apologizing."

She nodded and slid from his grip, climbing the staircase to the second floor.

He took a deep breath and headed back to Evan at the equipment room. "Did they get in at all?"

"Not that we can tell. I did a search before I came back here. Her room is clear."

Haiden nodded and stepped into the room, gathering his rifle. "What tipped you off?"

"The call about the riot. It was some kind of organized mob from an online ad. They were a smoke screen. Once Jeff figured it out, we started calling and headed this way."

Haiden slammed the locker door shut. "I'm done running from the people doing this. We need to cinch it up. Either it's about us as a group, or just Dani. The incident with Kyra isn't just a coincidence."

"I agree. But nothing connects all the events together. The attacks on Danica after Roltz threatened her—it all lines up. But Kyra's attack ... that's a different story. It doesn't fit. It's a different truck."

"Has Buck started looking through that footage?"

Evan shrugged. "You'd have to ask."

Haiden pushed past Evan to the back door. He was done worrying if they were coming after Danica. He trained for offense, and he was going to start right now. Danica would not be a target anymore.

32

D anica sat on the edge of the tub, sobbing.

It was too much. Her fear of small spaces, the smell of dirt and outdoors, jumping at loud noises ...

It'd been years since she had those nightmares, but being in the safe room made everything else come to the surface. Her claustrophobia was a short-lived anxiety that left out after a few years of therapy. Now, here she sat, embarrassed and nauseous.

"Good grief," she muttered as she wiped her face down with a wet washcloth.

Taking several deep breaths, she closed her eyes. "God, give me something here. I need some strength, some guidance. I can't go back there."

Starting the shower, she stripped down and stepped into the steam. Letting the water wash over her face and head, she closed her eyes.

"The Lord is my shepherd. I shall not want. He makes me lie down in green pastures and leads me besides still waters. He restoreth my soul," she whispered.

The clenching in her heart eased. The Lord's Shepherd prayer had always given her hope, cleared the fog in the darkness. It gave her a path other than the chaos her life had fallen into after the incident.

Fear had claimed her for way longer than she wanted to admit. The recent events wouldn't put her back in that place. It wouldn't happen ever again.

"WHAT'RE YOU DOING?"

Danica walked past Haiden and headed for the garage.

"Dani?"

"I want to talk to Buck, see what's going on."

Haiden pushed in front, making her pause. "Dani, go rest. You're exhausted."

"I am. I'm completely exhausted and sick of everything that keeps happening. I want to know who's behind this, and that starts with the faces we have on the cameras."

"Buck is fast, but he can't do miracles. We have to go through proper channels if we want to prosecute."

She crossed her arms and did her best to keep from falling into him. That was happening a lot lately.

"Hey, I know you want answers. We all do. Buck won't keep th-things from you. Neither will I."

"I know that. But I need to be in this. I can't sit around and wait for someone to come after us."

Haiden stepped forward, gently holding her elbow. "They lured our team out of the office, knowing you would be here. They're after you, not us."

"How could they know?"

He shrugged. "No idea. You need to be careful, be safe. Two-man teams. You're stuck with me."

His smirk pulled a smile out of her. Right now, in this moment, she didn't have a reason to smile. But she stood in front of him, unable to stop.

"Let me go grab Buck. You stay inside." His amazing eyes searched hers, and she nodded.

She leaned against the wall and waited as Haiden stepped outside. Staring at the equipment room in front of her, she blew out a deep breath.

"Dani?"

She barely glanced up before Bex grabbed her in a hug.

"I'm fine."

"I'm not so sure." Bexley stepped back and frowned. "You're attached to me. Looks like my protection skills are going to be useful sooner rather than later."

"Danica. Come on." Buck walked in and pulled at her elbow, guiding her down the hallway and to his office. "Have a seat."

"This feels all too familiar," she mumbled.

He had used that phrase for his many teachable moments throughout her life. Falling to the oversized chair in front of his desk, she pulled her legs up into the seat.

"We've sent several faces on to the police. I'll get a buddy of mine to run them through facial recognition. We'll get a match soon."

"You think this is about me? Or the team?"

Buck frowned, his jaw tensing. "Not sure."

"How could they know I was here? How could they know I wasn't with the team on the callout? I think Roltz is using some guys to make us look bad. They put those bombs there to cause a scene."

"Could be." He nodded and leaned into the desk. "That makes sense. Us running around like we don't know what we're doing, making us look bad to the press."

"What does Jeff think?"

Buck winced. "He's in a pretty bad mood. This kind of psychological game isn't one he enjoys."

"I thought that's why he went into profiling."

"Not when you're in the middle. With Kyra being attacked,

too, it's hitting far too close to home. Have you had any calls from Kyra?"

"No." She patted her back pocket and frowned. "I'm not even sure where that phone is you gave me. Probably in my room."

"This is a team situation, and I want everyone on alert. No one goes out alone. Got it?"

"Of course. I'm not looking to cause issues, I just don't ... this is pushing some buttons."

"Nightmares?"

She nodded, pulling at a string on her sweatshirt sleeve. "I had a slight meltdown in the safe room. Things have been off since everything with Kyra and getting hit by that truck. Maybe you should've taken me to get a scan."

Buck chuckled. "You're fine. I'm not worried about you, Dani."

"Maybe you should have that conversation with everyone else. Between Haiden and Bexley, I can't go to the bathroom without an escort."

"As long as it's Bex. If Haiden tries, we'll have issues."

She smiled at her uncle. "I think I need to take some time after all of this. Go be with Kyra and mom for a while."

"Why don't you go now?"

"I'm not leaving, not until we figure this out and put Roltz in his place."

Buck stood and walked around the desk, leaning on the edge in front of her. "It might not be him."

"What? Everything points to him and his threats."

"That's it. He's too smart to let it all come back to him. The guy's a jerk, and I want nothing to do with him, but he's smart enough to build an empire. He wouldn't threaten you or us, and then go about trying to discredit us."

"But you just said that makes sense."

"It does. I think there's another mastermind behind this, but I don't know who."

A quick rap sounded on the door, and Jeff walked in. "Hey, you okay?"

She nodded as Jeff took a seat on the armrest of her chair. "I'm fine. I mean, I'm not injured or anything."

Jeff frowned. "The police have all the evidence from the doors and are headed out."

"Captain DeSalis call yet?"

Jeff shook his head. "Too soon. Comparing those images is going to take some time."

Buck walked back around to his desk and sat down. Pulling out his laptop, he slid a flash drive into the port.

"What's that?" She leaned on her knee.

"Pictures," Buck said.

"You kept copies of the pictures?" Jeff stood and walked around the desk. "DeSalis won't like that."

"The only way he finds out is if these pictures make their way into the public. That won't happen. Besides, my guys are faster. I bet I get a name before DeSalis can even log them into the police system."

"Why's the captain here? Why not Sutton?"

Buck shrugged and glanced up at her. "DeSalis said this kind of attack should go to the feds, but he wants to handle it in house. They're trying to keep a lid on the attack and the demonstration we crashed. It's not looking great."

She sighed and leaned back in the seat.

"We'll figure it out, Dani. Don't worry."

She nodded at Jeff. "How did you know?"

"The online post. It read like any other post until it got to the words 'Total Request Team effort.' The letters *TRT* were capitalized."

"So, someone wanted us to figure it out?"

Jeff straightened from the computer. "I think someone wanted us to go in guns blazing and cause a scene. DeSalis told me Sergeant Sutton found speakers set up around the square.

They were aimed toward the building, so the sound would bounce off."

"What sound?"

"Gunshots."

Her jaw dropped. "Seriously? Someone could've been hurt."

"Exactly. Whoever set this up wanted chaos, wanted someone to shoot, or the people to go to the media and say they were being shot at either by a lone gunman or even by us. This is a smear campaign."

"Then why attack us?" she asked.

Jeff sighed. "I don't know. I don't have a clear picture of what's going on. I feel like it'll all make sense when we catch whoever is behind this. And that starts once we ID these guys who planted the bombs."

Jeff was right. They needed to discover what their attacker was hoping to accomplish. She wanted it to stop and Roltz—or whoever it was—to be taken down. Now.

33

D anica tapped away on Buck's laptop, looking through the traffic camera footage.

"Dani?"

She frowned at Haiden's voice. "I had hoped you would all be busy." She glanced up.

"What'd you find?" Haiden walked around the desk to stand next to her.

"This is the video from when I was hit." She pushed play, and the footage rolled.

Her car drove through two traffic lights, then a white truck materialized behind her.

"No view of the tags?"

"I've tried everything, but there's no shot that gives us anything besides this image." She froze the frame. "It's a GMC, white, but I'm not a car person, and I don't know what model or anything. Not that it would help—there are probably thousands of the same kind out there."

Haiden leaned in, and she shifted. His cologne wafted around her, and she wished for another nap on the couch. Although him seeing her fly off after a nightmare was an embarrassment. And then there was the scene in the equipment room ...

"You're right about there being a lot of them in the city. We need to see the driver's face."

"I can't zoom in. It distorts the picture."

"Did the video of you and Jeff have anything different?"

"Very different." She put the picture of the truck that attacked her and Jeff on the screen. "A red truck."

"Like the first time you were hit."

"Exactly. Two different trucks. Two different attack methods. The first truck just bumped me, but in this video, it looks like it's going to slam into us. See how the driver turns the wheel? I think he was trying to sideswipe us, but Jeff reacted quicker, throwing us out of the way."

"Okay. And the white one?"

She frowned. "He's head-on, full-blown attack mode. He slammed into Krya's car so hard, it wedged it into a tree. I think he was planning something worse for me." She clicked on the video and enlarged the frame. "Look here, to the right." She motioned to the corner.

"A concrete barrier?"

"Yeah. I think he was aiming for that. But I got ahead, and then instead of turning, I went straight. He was hoping I'd turn right so he could slam me into it."

"Play it again."

She hit play. After the light, the truck swung wide left while she went straight.

"I think you're right." Haiden sat on the edge of the desk, facing her. "Buck thought he could get a plate number from the stores."

"Nothing yet."

"And the faces?"

She shrugged and pulled them up to scroll through, attempting to ignore Haiden watching her. "I don't recognize any of them. Have you looked?"

He shook his head.

"You see something?"

"Nope," she mumbled.

Buck came into the office.

"You don't have any messages on here about names or tags."

"I just got one. Move." Buck prodded her from the chair and sat. "I've got a name, and I want to see if we can tie him to anyone we know."

She stepped out of the way. Haiden took hold of her waist, pulling her back.

"Um, no tags?" she asked.

"No. Not having any luck, but I think this is better, anyway. Chances are those trucks are stolen. Name is Adil Harrison. Sound familiar?"

Shaking her head at Buck's question, she ignored Haiden leaning in from behind.

"Why don't you go rest?" Haiden whispered in her ear.

Gripping her arms across her chest, she forced herself to not shudder. "I want to see how it connects."

"Go lie down, Dani. This might take a while." Buck motioned her out.

"Fine," she mumbled.

Haiden escorted her from the office. "Have you heard from Kyra?"

"Yeah. I called her earlier." Instead of going upstairs, she ignored Haiden's huff and went to the couch. "She's feeling better, but with her history, they're limited with what they can give her for pain. She said it's been hard to handle when it hurts, but everyone's been really nice and doing what they can for her."

"Has she always been a find the bright side person?"

Danica chuckled as Haiden sat on the ottoman in front of her. "Not really. But after rehab, she went through some tough times. Mom and some women at church rallied around her and helped her get through it. She credits them with keeping her sane."

Her smile faded. Her mother had insisted she come and help

Kyra, but Danica couldn't make herself be a part of it all. The guilt was too much as it was.

"Don't do that," Haiden squeezed her leg. "I can tell you're blaming yourself for something."

She frowned. How could he see right through her?

"Kyra made her own path. So did you. God has a path for everyone."

"That's what my mom said," she whispered, staring up at him. "Sometimes, not very often, she is lucid, and I can talk to her. It doesn't always last long, but when she's present, it's almost normal again."

He slid into the couch next to her, wrapping her up. She wiped her face and took a deep breath.

"Have you talked to your dad today?"

"No. I'm not ... I'm not there yet." He sighed. "I told him the other day I would try. I mean, I want to let it go."

"I'm sure you do."

He took up her hand and pulled it to his chest. "I wanted to tell you, I think—"

Jeff walked in and sat in the recliner. "Buck has a hunch."

Haiden's jaw clenched.

She eyed Jeff. "What hunch?"

"Not sure. But he's got something on his mind. He's making sure Sutton knows about it."

"You really think making Sutton mad is a good idea?" Haiden grumbled. He lowered her hand down to the couch and released it.

She crossed her arms. It was bad enough that he always turned away, but refusing to hold her hand in front of Jeff? Really?

"Thompson." Buck walked in, phone to his ear.

"Send me the details. Be there in less than ten." Buck motioned to them. "Where are Bex and Evan?"

"In the garage, working on hand to hand." Jeff stood.

"Go get them. We need to roll. There's a call in about a kidnapping."

"A kidnapping?"

Buck nodded. Danica and Haiden followed him to the equipment room.

"Sutton said the commissioner asked us to get there now. It's a few miles outside the city, and the police are tied up with a major pileup on the freeway. We've got to help with the search."

Danica grabbed her vest from the equipment room, and Haiden put his hand out.

"I'm going."

Haiden frowned. "It's not safe."

"So, I stay here alone? If there's a missing kid, we all go."

Haiden let out a huff and gathered his equipment. Jeff slapped Haiden's shoulder as he passed by, then pulled Danica in front of him to the SUV.

Once everyone was loaded into the SUV, Buck backed out and flipped on the sirens, accelerating toward the freeway.

"Possible sighting of kidnapped child. Proceed with caution, suspect considered armed and dangerous." Jeff read the text out loud as his finger tapped on the stock of the rifle.

She frowned. "What's wrong now?"

Jeff turned from the passenger seat to look back at her. "This isn't right."

"You think someone is luring us again? With the report of a kidnapped child?"

He sighed. "We can't turn down a kidnapping case. It's a nightmare PR situation, but we have to be concerned about a trap. Especially after what happened downtown and the fact the protesters came to the office." His eyes narrowed as his jaw tightened.

Danica shrugged. "Hey, what did I do?"

"You don't go anywhere alone, got it?" Buck demanded.

"Number one, that's the deal for the entire team. Number two, this is about the TRT, not me."

"I don't care. Something doesn't make sense, and I think it's more about you than about us."

She huffed.

"She's not going anywhere alone," Haiden said.

Jeff cut his eyes toward Haiden and nodded.

Haiden's hand gripped hers, pulling it to his leg. As much as she didn't want to believe she needed help, having him beside her, holding on, was a welcome distraction.

34

Danica slid from the SUV, Haiden at her heels. He pulled her to a stop.

"We're supposed to team up, not be attached at the hip."

Haiden kept his hand firmly on her waist, giving a squeeze as he leaned in. With his hat pulled down low, he narrowed his eyes from under the bill. "I'm not getting any farther than this," he mumbled. "I hope that's okay."

She refused to shiver. "Just don't get in the way of my gun once we go in." Turning away from Haiden and those eyes of his, she marched up to Buck. "Where do we go?"

Buck peered between her and Haiden, his jaw tense. "We're waiting on police this time. No one goes in unless I say. Got it?" He eyed the rest of the team. "This is a possible kidnapping, so we're looking for anyone in or around this area. They might even hide outside the building."

"According to Sutton, the caller wasn't clear about who or what was here. Just a small child yelling and then an adult voice. The caller said the kid had on a red sweater, which matched the description of a small boy kidnapped from the area. Dani, you and Haiden go to the hill. I want eyes on the building, so when the police arrive, we've got the sit-rep ready, and we can follow them in."

"Are they on their way?" Jeff straightened his ear-com.

"Sutton's en route, two minutes."

She nodded and followed Haiden.

The SUV was parked several feet from the road, out of sight from the building, so Danica and Haiden climbed to the top of a small ridge. Skulking to the top, she peered over and got a good look at the old quarry. It sat in a low ravine, with several roads leading in and out of the area. She could see the steep and curved pathways that wrapped around the hills.

Haiden set up his rifle, and she crouched down beside him, stifling a shiver from the cool breeze. Pulling her thermal imaging monocular from her backpack, she searched the area.

"There's nothing here. I don't see any heat signatures," she said.

"If there's a kid, he or she might not show a signal. Keep watch, and be ready to move," Buck responded through the com.

As they sat, she rotated hands, shaking out her fists and forcing her focus on the scene. Haiden's hand gripped hers, and she jumped. Staring down, his green eyes shone upward.

Giving her fingers a squeeze, he went back to his scope.

"Car approaching. Looks like the police." Jeff's voice sounded.

She angled in the direction they had parked, finding Buck meeting with Sutton. Buck had removed his earpiece, so she couldn't hear their conversation.

"Where is everyone?" Haiden asked.

It was then she realized there were no other officers. No van with equipment or police tactical team following Sutton into the area. If this were a report of a kidnapped kid or a possible location of a kid, several dozen officers would arrive.

"Everyone, come in," Buck's gritty voice sounded over the com.

"That's so weird." She pulled out her com, staring at the empty building.

"What?" Haiden sat up next to her, his rifle across his lap.

"What if Jeff's right, and someone is trying to lure us here?"

"Why?"

"We know someone is trying to discredit us. With the attack on the office ... the trucks that seem to follow us around. We're missing something."

"So, you think we're being played?"

She turned at Haiden's deep voice. "I think we should see what's waiting in that building."

Haiden sighed and stuck the com back in his ear. "We need to clear it."

She pushed her earpiece back in just in time to hear Buck's irritated voice say, "What do you know?"

Haiden turned to her. "Dani needs to stay back, and we need to clear it."

"Get down here. Now." Buck demanded.

She huffed. "It's my idea. I want to help."

"You're the one Roltz is targeting. You're the one who's being attacked. You're not going in that building."

She walked down the hillside, pulling away from Haiden. "I can handle myself."

"We know that, but we also want you to be safe."

Refusing to argue, she glanced up at the looming tower of the quarry.

What if the situation were much more than it seemed?

HAIDEN WRAPPED an arm around Danica as they walked down to the building. Whatever was going on, she wasn't going to get caught in the middle.

Sutton stood waiting. "We traced the caller, and it came up as a Thomas Eller."

"That name's familiar. He's a contact for one of the men we ID'd who attacked our office."

Sutton nodded. "That's why we think this is another hoax. The description doesn't fit any child who's been abducted in this area that we know of. I've got some guys on standby, just in case, but my guess is there's something in that warehouse that's supposed to make a fool out of someone."

Buck frowned. "Then we get in there and get some evidence to prosecute whoever is wasting our time."

"What about Dani?" Haiden asked.

"Danica, stay here with Sutton. You're not going in that building."

"Buck."

"I'm serious. Someone is looking to make a point, and so far, they've centered on you."

Danica let out a sigh, but nodded.

"Stay close. We do this right." Buck motioned toward the building, and Evan took point.

"I'll be right back. Don't go anywhere," Haiden mumbled in her ear, then he hustled to catch up to the team.

Jeff held open the door. Evan went in first. Haiden followed, and Buck, Bexley, and Jeff came in behind. Following through the corridor, Haiden swept to the left, and Evan went right. The dark warehouse was empty, absent of the crates or debris that normally littered abandoned places like this.

They fanned out through each floor, clearing the building a section at a time. There were no rooms or closets to search through, making their work go fast.

"It's clear. I don't think anyone has been here in a long time." Evan turned on his helmet light, and they all followed suit.

Haiden scanned the area, heading toward the end of the fourth floor. Buck entered from clearing the far side and stopped short.

"Buck?"

"Someone's been here."

"Who?" Haiden stepped forward at Buck's voice.

On the ground lay a pair of purple running shoes.

"Get to Danica. Now!"

35

P acing the area, Danica's arms trembled as she hugged her body, trying to warm herself.

"You know what's going on?"

She turned to Sergeant Sutton. "No idea. You think this is all a hoax?"

He shrugged. "I think someone is working hard to mess things up for either you or for us. This callout, the last one downtown—it's like we're running in circles."

"But why?" She shook her head. "Tell me the truth. Are the police upset with us for helping?"

"No one I know." He stared at the building for a moment. "You want to wait in the car? I can turn on the heat."

"Sure."

Sliding into the passenger seat, she let out a sigh as Sutton started the engine and blasted the hot air, pointing the vents toward her.

"What's taking so long for them to clear it? It's not that big."

"They must've found something they didn't like." Sutton turned to her, narrowing his eyes. "You don't look like I pictured you."

She focused on the officer next to her and raised her eyebrow. "What does that mean? How do you know me?"

"I don't. Not really."

A blast of air hit her face, and she coughed, straining to take in a breath. Grasping for anything, she yanked on the door handle. It wouldn't open. Her world spun. She closed her eyes and disappeared into the darkness.

"DANI!" Haiden sprinted after the police car as it raced down the road, dust and debris flying up in its wake.

"Let's go." Buck grabbed his arm, and they piled into the SUV. "Call it in. If there's an officer involved, then we need to go through the right channels."

Haiden could hear Buck's voice on the phone, but the words didn't register. "Wh-what would he want with h-her?"

"Get me Commissioner Stonewell, now!" Buck shouted into the phone.

The engine revved, and Jeff cut the wheel. The SUV drifted around the corner on the dirt road. A cloud of dust swirled ahead of them. Jeff pushed to the left, trying to get around the debris cloud.

"Is that them?" Haiden leaned forward from the back seat.

"We're about to find out," Jeff said.

The engine roared, and the dust cloud cleared.

"Jeff! Stop!"

Haiden braced as Buck yelled. The SUV skidded to a stop, and Haiden caught himself before he flew into the dash.

"That was close."

Haiden sat up to see what Jeff was talking about. The edge of the road had a drop off. The dust cloud could've led them down an embankment.

Jeff stepped out of the SUV, and Haiden followed.

"He knew ..." Haiden mumbled, his heart in his throat.

"He's been here. He planned this. All the roads in and out—it's dangerous, and he knew we'd follow." Jeff's face reddened. He paced until Buck came from around the SUV.

"You guys okay?" Evan slid down from the other vehicle.

"No." Haiden fisted his hands. "We need to catch them."

"DeSalis can track the cruiser, and he's got a group of officers waiting to intercept."

"We should be there too," Haiden said, as he climbed back into the SUV. Jeff followed.

"DeSalis will keep us updated." Buck slid into the seat. "Head into town, and he'll let us know when they get him."

Haiden's leg bounced up and down, his head pounding. The police would stop Sutton. They must get to him. Stop him before he got away with Danica.

"Who is Sutton? Why did he take her?" Jeff asked.

Buck shook his head. "There's something else."

"Doesn't matter. It doesn't matter w-why. Let's just find him and get her back." Haiden's hands fisted. "I can't believe we thought it would be okay to leave her alone while we cleared that place."

"It was the best idea at the time. We had no information otherwise." Buck took a deep breath. "But DeSalis has Sutton's car. We'll get answers soon."

Pulling onto the highway, Buck's phone went off.

"Thompson."

Haiden leaned forward.

"What? How did that happen? No, I don't want an excuse. We're on our way."

"Fine, but I want a call as soon as you have him." Buck flung the phone to the dash.

"What's going on?" Jeff's eyes darted between the road and Buck.

"He took out the tracker and put it on a different cruiser."

"What?" Haiden struggled to swallow. "Tell me they have a trace on his phone."

"They're working on it." Buck hung his head. "But if Sutton thought ahead to move the tracker from the cruiser, I'm not getting my hopes up for the phone. Head to the police station."

"The station? We need to search the area, see if we can get a direction." Jeff argued.

"The police are on it. We need to give our statement ASAP so they can get past us and on to the next step." Buck stated.

Haiden shook his head, irritation building "The next step ... is shutting everything down, and put Sutton's name and face out there."

Buck turned in the seat to face Haiden. "I know. Trust me. But I have no doubt this guy didn't think of everything. He's in a police cruiser—he can't hide forever."

36

Danica's head spun. A soft moan left her lips.

"Shut up!"

Shouting and scuffling echoed. The growing noises made her head throb even more.

"I won't let this happen!"

She struggled to open her eyes, but her head bobbed, and she fell forward. Her arms pulled from behind her. They burned as she tugged, her wrists stung at the hard plastic digging into her skin.

Three shots sounded..

Wake up. You have to wake up!

Heart pounding, she struggled against the lethargy overwhelming her body. Taking a deep breath, an acrid smell filled her nostrils, smothering her. She tried to cough, but her senses shut down once more.

HAIDEN'S WORLD spun out of control. He paced the TRT office.

Bexley's sobs echoed in the background, Evan's voice trying to soothe her.

"I want answers, now." Jeff stood at the window, shouting into the phone before he slammed it on the table.

"I can't ... can't sit here and do nothing."

"Haiden." Jeff's voice rang empty.

Haiden needed to get out of here. If he headed back to the scene, maybe he could find a track, a trail to where the police cruiser disappeared. There were several roads in and out of that place. Maybe he could find something.

"Haiden."

He turned at Buck's voice.

Buck stood in the hallway, his face twisted as he shoved the phone in his back pocket. "That was Captain DeSalis. Sergeant Sutton is AWOL, and the callout to the warehouse was never approved through any channels. He also affirmed that Sutton isn't his real last name. It changed ten years ago when he was legally adopted by his mother's family. His real last name is Barnett."

"Eugene Barnett?" Jeff murmured. "He killed Tony's mom."

"What?" Bexley's voice rose.

Buck only nodded. "Oscar Sutton is really Oscar Barnett, the son of Eugene, who tried to kill Danica nearly fifteen years ago."

37

Jeff's heart pounded in his ears as he stared blankly at Buck.

"W-we need to find Tony."

"Didn't you just hear him?" Jeff hissed at Haiden. "This is the son of the guy who tried to kill Dani years ago. Eugene Barnett killed Tony's mom. It has nothing to do with Tony."

"He's Tony's cousin, right? You think Tony doesn't know w-where the guy is or who he is?"

Pacing away from Haiden, Jeff yanked his phone free and called Tony.

"Hey, man. What's up?"

"Have you seen Dani recently?"

"We talked for a bit yesterday. She was pretty upset about that Haiden guy. I'm not sure what's going on there, but it's weird."

Jeff put a glare on Haiden as he paced back and forth. "Yeah, it is."

"Is something wrong? You want me to come over?"

"No. I mean ... I don't know." Jeff raked his fingers through his hair. "I need to ask you something."

"You're scaring me, Jeff. What's going on?"

"Have you heard about your cousin?"

"What cousin?"

"Oscar."

Silence filled the moment.

"What about him?" Tony whispered.

"He's a police officer here in Dallas. We've been in contact with him, but he's using a different name."

"What are you trying to say? Is Danica in trouble?"

"I don't know—"

"I'm headed that way."

Jeff shook his head. "Tony."

"This is all your fault! After what happened to Kyra, how could you just let her run around like everything was fine?"

"Tony."

The line cut out, and Jeff clenched the phone in his fist. "I can't believe this," he mumbled.

"What'd he say?"

Jeff glared at Buck. "He's one of our closest friends and is worried for Dani. Especially now that I pointed out his cousin is in town and causing trouble."

"H-he didn't know?" Haiden's face turned bright red.

"Of course not." Jeff stepped into Haiden's face. "I'm not sure where this jealousy is coming from. Especially since you missed the bus on that with Dani. You don't have a right to act as if you have any idea what's going on. You weren't there. You didn't see what it did to Tony and to Danica."

Evan pushed a hand between them, and Jeff stepped back.

"Then explain it."

Jeff cut his eyes to Evan before going back to Haiden. "I got a phone call from Kyra, hysterical. She said someone killed Dani, and Buck was on his way to find them."

"What?" Bexley's shriek echoed.

"Why was Buck there?"

Shaking his head at Evan, Jeff paced a moment. "Buck is Dani's uncle. He was there when her father died." He glanced up at a red-faced Buck. "I went over there, and by then, there were police cars everywhere, and Tony and his sister had just pulled in. I found Kyra and tried to calm her down. Buck came out of the woods, holding onto the gurney, and Danica was passed out."

"Oh my," Bexley exclaimed. "What happened?"

Jeff nodded to Buck.

"Kyra said they had been exploring an old house across the field from theirs. Someone chased them into the woods. I had just pulled into their driveway and heard a gunshot. Kyra came up and told me had happened. By the time I got there, Dani was out cold, wrapped in a blanket, and lying in an unfilled grave."

Swallowing the bile burning his throat, Jeff paced as Buck continued.

"The man had already killed Tony's mom and had just finished burying her. I made it before he got to Dani. Danica told me later it was the shoes. She saw the purple shoes Tony's mom always wore. They were the same as the shoes in that warehouse."

"And Tony?"

Jeff glanced at Haiden, then peered at Evan. "His life ended. He and his sister were everywhere on the news, and they both stopped coming to school. They got bullied tirelessly, and Dani felt it was all her fault."

"It wasn't," Haiden mumbled.

"I know that, and Tony knows that. He tells her all the time. Even now. So, for you to think he has anything to do with his cousin, you're wrong."

"Why do you think Tony would know?" Evan stood toe to toe with Haiden.

"He's h-his cousin, his family. There's no way he knows nothing about him or the fact he's now in town. Sutton's father ruined Tony's life. Don't you think he'd keep track of him?"

Buck lifted his phone and headed down the hallway. "They think they have video of Sutton. Let's go."

Jeff followed Buck from the living room and crowded into the SUV with everyone else.

"Did they see Dani?"

"No," Buck grumbled.

Jeff clenched his jaw as his hand tightened around his phone. Opening it up, he texted Tony.

> We're on our way to where Oscar was last seen. I'll keep you updated.

Nothing better happen to her.

> She's smart and strong. We both know she's survived worse.

You better let me know the second you find her. I mean it.

Jeff exhaled a deep breath.

> I will.

God, please protect her. Let us get to Sutton first.

38

"Buck?" Haiden's heart pounded at the sight of the ambulance and police roadblock.

"Just wait," Buck whispered.

Sliding from the SUV, Haiden observed Buck and Jeff trying to get information from the officer at the yellow police tape.

"Let me ask. Just hang on." The officer spoke into his radio. "I have the TRT here waiting."

"They're good," a scratchy voice came over the radio.

The officer nodded his head and pulled up the tape. Rushing past the officers lining the building, a man in a suit stopped them at the entrance.

"Captain DeSalis." Buck nodded.

"She's not here. There's no evidence she was here, but the crime unit is sweeping his car and the building."

"W-what do you mean she's not here?"

"Haiden." Jeff took Haiden's arm.

Ignoring Jeff, Haiden pushed into the captain's space. "Where is she? Is h-he here?"

"He is. But he's not talking." DeSalis nodded to the body bag being wheeled out on a gurney. "Double tap to the heart, close range."

"Weapon?" Buck muttered.

"Nothing's been found so far. We're pulling video from surrounding buildings and intersections, trying to pinpoint when he arrived and if anyone was following him."

"How did he get this far?" Jeff's arms crossed as he glared at the captain. "This can't be his first offense. You don't just decide one day to kidnap someone."

"As you know, this isn't just someone," DeSalis said through gritted teeth. "But Sutton has a clean record. Not even a reprimand in his file. He's always been a stand-up officer."

"He kidnapped her," Haiden grumbled. "We all saw him drive off with her, then evade contact. This was premeditated. Wh-what about the shoes?"

"Look, I'm not saying he's not behind all this. But he's dead, and we don't know what happened. Once he found out who she was, maybe he wanted to talk and then things went bad."

"You think Dani did that?" Jeff's voice rose above the chaos of the scene as he pointed at the gurney being wheeled away. "If she had, she'd have found a way to make contact."

DeSalis held out his hands. "We don't know what happened. Until we figure that out, I'm not ready to label anyone a killer."

Haiden turned to pace, anger and frustration getting the best of him.

"If Dani had to defend herself, she would've."

He nodded at Jeff's comment. "But she w-would've called."

"Spread out. See what you can see." Buck barked orders, trying to maintain the situation.

Head down, Haiden followed instructions and wandered the scene. The downtown warehouse was a perfect place to hide. With the loud traffic noise and echoing buildings—even if a gunshot sounded, no one would hear.

The back of the building was crawling with technicians, all examining the police cruiser tucked into the crevice between the buildings.

Haiden swallowed the lump forming in his throat. After

everything they'd talked about, avoided, it was becoming clearer and clearer that a life without Danica wasn't what he wanted. It wasn't just fear of her being in danger. It was the fear that the one person in the world he wanted a future with could be fighting for her life.

"Over here." Evan called.

He ducked under the crime scene tape and went to the open field.

"There are tire tracks here. And blood, here." Evan pointed to the ruts in the tall grass. A few reddish drops were scattered among the weeds. "I think whoever shot Sutton had a car waiting or maybe even drove it here."

"Then took Danica," Haiden whispered.

Evan nodded.

"Techs are on their way." Jeff stood over the ruts, his face pale. "Those are wide tracks, a truck or SUV?"

"Yeah." Haiden followed the tracks to where the field ended and the road began. Muddy impressions turned right, and Haiden walked the road where they led.

Run-down homes and winter trees lined the sides. The ice-cold wind chilled his face.

"God, let her be safe. Lead me to her. Please don't let this be the end." His prayer hollow, he paused at the corner. A check-cashing storefront sported several video cameras pointed outward. Pulling out his phone, he called Buck.

"Follow the tracks. There's a storefront with video cameras."

"On my way."

Not willing to wait, Haiden entered the store.

"Can I help you?"

"I need to see the video from those cameras."

The middle-aged woman frowned as she leaned into the counter. "You got a warrant?"

"Not yet." He stepped closer. "I need to know about the truck that came flying down through here about an hour ago."

"Honey, you don't need video for that. Some guy in a white

truck whipped through here like he was on fire." She shrugged. "Hopped the curb out in front."

"Did you see the plates?"

"Nope—just the driver."

"W-what'd he look like?"

She pulled out a package of gum from below the counter. "White guy, dark hair. Couldn't really see his face. It was too fast."

"Anyone else inside?"

Chomping loudly on her gum, the woman furrowed her brows. "Maybe. I couldn't tell what was on the passenger side. I just remember seeing him."

"Him who?" Buck questioned from the doorway.

"Thanks. You might want to get that video out," Haiden said as he took off from the store.

"Warrant will be here in five for the video." Buck's voice came from behind. "What did she say?"

"Wh-white guy with black hair. White truck."

"White truck? Like what hit Kyra and Dani, but not Dani and me?" Jeff asked.

"What did Tony say earlier?" Buck questioned.

"You too?" Jeff let out an exasperated breath. "I can't believe this. Oscar Sutton, Burnett, whatever his name is, has you all fooled. He's got a partner, and we need to figure it out."

"We *are* trying to figure out who the partner is. Think outside the box and see what other options there are. Tony might still know more than he's saying. He's the only person we know who has any connection to Sutton. We cover all bases. Got it?"

Jeff's eyes cut behind Haiden for a second before he started pacing.

"Someone convinced Sutton to risk his career to lure us around town, making us appear incompetent. Whoever it was, they were able to manipulate, then kill him.. Otherwise, it makes no sense. Tony might know something about the men he'd been in contact with or where he hung out."

"I'm telling you, Tony was just as shocked as we were. There's no way he had any contact or could tell us anything about Oscar or who he was in contact with."

"What about the mayor guy? Roltz?" Bexley had a grip on Evan's arm, her eyes and cheeks red. "We thought maybe it was about him too. Could he be responsible?"

Jeff shrugged. "I'd put my money on Roltz. He's got access to the commissioner and a lot of money to throw around. If he were to find out who Oscar really was, it wouldn't be hard to connect the dots. The guy is looking to destroy us. Taking out one of our own would do it."

"Let me make a phone call." Buck stepped from the group.

"We'll get her back, Bex." Evan wrapped Bexley up in a hug.

Haiden's heart ached. In all his life, the best hug he'd ever had was with Danica hanging on to him. Then he'd walked away.

"Fine." Buck hung up and marched back to the group. "DeSalis is on his way with the warrant, but unless it's a perfectly clear picture, which I doubt, it'll take some time to clean it up enough to get a positive ID. While we wait on that, I've got a meeting with Roltz."

"How did you manage that?" Evan asked.

"I've still got some pull in this town," Buck answered.

Haiden nodded. "I'm going."

"No," Jeff said.

Haiden glared.

"You can't go in there attacking him. He *wants* a fight. If it is him, he's got someone else doing his dirty work. No way he gets his hands dirty while he's put in a bid for mayor. We go in there guns blazing, and he'll have more ammo to destroy us."

"I don't care about this job," Haiden said.

"Jeff's right. Dani is the priority here, not our jobs." Buck crossed his arm. "But this has to be handled the right way if we're going to get anything out of Roltz. I'll let you know as soon as we get out of the meeting."

Haiden's face heated. "I can't just do nothing."

"Let's help canvas," Bexley commented. "I'm sure we can ask about a white truck, maybe even show Dani's picture around. If she was in the truck, someone had to see her."

Haiden paced back and forth, his heart pounding in his chest. "I'm going back to the scene, see if I can find tracks, something to give us a lead. Call if you find anything."

He took off to the SUV, flagging Buck down before they could leave.

"Drop me off at the office," Haiden said, as he climbed into the back. "I'll take my Jeep back to the scene and see if I can find anything."

"Sounds good. Keep your phone on. We'll call when we know something."

He aimlessly nodded at Buck, staring out the window at the cool weather rolling in.

God, protect her where I've failed. I never should've left her side.

39

"Have a seat, gentlemen."

Jeff frowned as Louis Roltz sat down with a large grin across his face. Instead of facing them alone, Roltz had called in a lawyer.

"Is there a reason for the legal protection?" Jeff asked.

Roltz shrugged. "Just trying to keep myself from being framed."

"Louis, that's enough. Let me do the talking." The lawyer shifted in his seat. "My name is Guy Yates. I'm Mr. Roltz's legal advisor. What is this meeting about?"

"We've been targeted lately, and after Mr. Roltz's comments at our last meeting, we have concerns."

"I can assure you, my client has no intentions of threatening anyone."

Buck's jaw twitched. "Actually, he's already threatened someone. And now, she's been kidnapped."

"What?" Roltz sat forward, his mouth dropped. "What're you talking about?"

"Danica Freeman is missing. She's been kidnapped. You sat right there when you told her to be careful in this dangerous city."

The lawyer stared at Roltz. "Gentlemen, I think it's time you leave." Yates stood and buttoned his jacket. "My client has nothing else to say."

Buck walked around the table.

"Buck?"

Buck ignored Jeff and stood toe to toe with Roltz.

"If you threaten my client—"

"Quiet." Buck's deep voice echoed in the large room. "If something happens to her, I'll be bringing up charges against you for your threats. You'll never see the inside of the mayoral office."

"Is that a threat?" Yates scoffed.

"I don't make threats." Buck turned and walked away.

Roltz remained silent, but his face reddened.

"Gentlemen." Jeff nodded and followed Buck from the room.

In the parking lot, Jeff reached the driver's side first and slid in.

"Why're you driving?" Buck asked as he got inside.

"I think I'm better equipped at the moment." He started up the vehicle and headed for the office. "Want to explain what all that was?"

"He didn't do it."

"What?"

Buck turned to him. "He was in shock. He had no idea she was missing."

"But that's impossible. Someone is still targeting us. Who else could it be?"

"Kyra is the key. She was the first domino in this entire thing." Buck pulled out his phone and put it on Bluetooth.

"Riley." The voice rang out through the SUV's speakers.

"It's Buck."

"How's it going?"

Buck clenched his jaw before responding. "Not good. I need to know who attacked Kyra. Now."

"I don't have that information. We've pulled some video, but nothing definite."

"A white truck?"

"Sure. That's what we've been looking for. What's going on Buck?"

"Someone's taken Dani."

"What?"

Jeff clenched the steering wheel.

"We've had some attacks on our team, but I think it was centered on Danica. Kyra's accident was made to unnerve her, make her vulnerable. When that didn't happen, they moved on to more drastic measures. I need that truck. Now."

"Let me see what I can do. I just can't believe ..."

"What is it, Riley?" Jeff asked.

"Jeff? Jeff Powers?"

"Yeah, it's me. I can tell you've got something on your mind. Tell me."

Riley hesitated. "It's nothing serious."

"Dani's missing. Whatever you've got on your mind, I want to know," Buck demanded.

"Things have been off here. That fire wasn't the first we've had in the last week. The house across the field—"

"Wait, the house where Tony's mom was killed burned?"

"To the ground. There's nothing left. A large tree had fallen across the driveway. We couldn't get a fire truck in there quick enough. It was dry and went up like a shot."

Jeff's heart pounded. "Riley, is Eugene Burnett still in prison?"

"Far as I know. Why? You think this has to do with him?"

Jeff opened his mouth, but nothing came out. It just couldn't be true. If Eugene was still in prison, what other living person would hold that kind of grudge?

"Jeff?"

"Thanks, Riley. Give me a call when you get that license plate. I've got some friends who can work fast."

"Will do. Hope you find her. That girl deserves a happy ending."

Silence enveloped the car.

"You thinking what I'm thinking?" Jeff whispered.

"Who had a reason to hate the Freeman girls and is still alive and walking around free?"

"Are we absolutely certain it's Oscar Sutton in that body bag?" Jeff turned to Buck.

Buck shrugged. "DeSalis has no reason to lie about it. But we can always verify."

"Let's go to the morgue. I want to see his face. To know he's no longer a threat."

"Agreed."

HAIDEN WALKED around the large warehouse, scanning the ground for something, anything, that could give them a lead.

His phone vibrated.

No luck on the canvas.

A lot of people remembered seeing the white truck, but no one spotted someone else inside.

Swallowing the bile building in his throat, he shook his head and paused. Hanging his hands on his hips, he sucked in a deep breath.

"This can't be h-happening," he whispered.

Going to a knee, he rested his head on his raised knee.

"God, please, just give me this one thing. I never asked for more once I left that house. You gave me a future, a life, and it's all I ever wanted. But for the first time, I want more than to merely survive. I want something good in this life. Danica deserves much more, but I ... I want h-her."

He'd never asked God for more than a family, a future. God

got him out of his house and gave him a future. Now, he just wanted, needed, a family. Danica was his family.

His phone vibrated again. Wiping his face, he pulled the phone free.

Get back to the office. Now.

Pushing off the ground, he stood and responded to Buck's text and shoved the phone back in his pocket. His heart pounding, he took a deep breath and headed back to his Jeep.

His Bluetooth went off as soon as he turned the engine over.

"Hello?"

"Haiden?"

He sighed. "Mom, I can't, not r-right now."

"Your dad wants to talk. Hang on."

"Mom," he let out a grunt as he buckled.

"Haiden?"

His skin pricked at the sound of his father's voice. "I can't really t-talk right now."

"I needed to tell you something. I read this and wanted you to hear it." His father's voice strained with heavy breaths.

"Yeah, o-okay."

"Have I not commanded you? Be strong and courageous. Do not be frightened, and do not be dismayed, for the Lord your God is with you wherever you go. Haiden, last time you were here, you said you were afraid of becoming me. Don't be frightened. God is with you. I have no doubts he'll pull you through whatever you end up facing."

Tears streaming down his cheeks, Haiden couldn't make himself speak.

A rustle in the line echoed in the car.

"Dad?"

"Haiden?" His mother's voice sounded. "Are you there?"

"Yeah. Is h-he okay?"

A door sounded in the background. "He started treatment

today, but it's not going well. Can you come by?"

Haiden swallowed the lump in his throat. "No, I can't. Dani —Danica is missing."

"Oh, no! I'm so sorry, Haiden. We'll be praying."

"Thanks, Mom."

"Be safe and call us when you find her."

"I will." He hung up the phone.

Gripping the wheel, he headed out the back way of the complex, hoping to spot some tire tracks on one of the roads that wound around the hillside. But with the tears still covering his eyes, he struggled to see.

"God, please help me find her. Protect her."

"Wake up, Dani."

A familiar voice echoed as Danica fought to engage her senses.

"I need you to wake up before it's too late."

Too late? What did that mean? Head aching, her body stiff and sore, she pried open her eyes. The blurry form of her boots came into view. Her ankles were zip-tied together, and her wrists were zip-tied as well.

"What ... what's going on?" Her mouth dry, she blinked to orient herself and tried to straighten.

"You ready?"

She turned her head, then closed her eyes. The motion made her sick.

"There's his car. You ready?"

She could barely make out the hand pointing as her eyes finally engaged. Haiden's white Jeep, with the KC lights on top, bumped and rocked down the road. Her mind snapped into gear.

Straining, the breath left her body as the Jeep suddenly lunged forward, missing the turn and careening off the side of the cliff.

40

J eff stood, staring at the covered body in the cool morgue.

"Thanks for this, Phil. I appreciate it." Buck walked in with a man in a white coat.

"Just don't let Dr. Phariss know I let you in without the police giving it the okay." Phil stepped up to the body and pulled the sheet back. "Well?"

Jeff frowned and glanced up at Buck. "Now what?"

Buck let out a breath. "This is definitely him. Now, we need to figure out why."

"HAIDEN?" Danica screamed as she pulled on her restraints. "What did you do?" Her shoulders burned as the Jeep disappeared into the ravine. She couldn't take her eyes off the place where Haiden's vehicle went over the edge.

"He was in the way."

"But Haiden ..."

"He deserved it. Guy was a jerk."

Her breath left her body, and she struggled to inhale. Haiden can't be dead. He can't be. Maybe it wasn't him in the Jeep. He would know how to survive, right? Her mind spun as the car backed up and then turned toward the road.

"Have you seen the X-rays of that guy? I mean ... man. I've never seen so many broken bones."

"Stop," she whispered.

Her heart burst as tears streamed down her face. She figured he'd been abused, but that ... no wonder he didn't want to talk about it. Her body ached and burned as she pulled against the zip ties that attached her wrists to the lever beneath her seat.

"I needed him out of the way."

Haiden had been right all along.

"WHERE'S HAIDEN?" Jeff paced the room, waiting for Buck to get off the phone.

"I thought Buck said he was on his way back?" Bexley sat at the island with another mug of coffee.

"He needs to get here. We'll be moving out just as soon as Buck clears it with Captain DeSalis."

Buck walked into the living room. "We're staying put."

"What? Are you kidding me?"

Buck lifted his hand. "Let me explain. DeSalis didn't pull Adil Garrison's name like we did. They traced the phone of Thomas Eller, the name that popped when he called in the phony kidnapping. He's a known associate of Adil's. They busted into an apartment and found two of the three men from the attack on our building dead."

"Both names we pinged are dead?" Jeff's jaw dropped.

"Yes. Adil and Thomas are both dead."

"Who's the third?" Evan asked.

"Dale Fletcher."

"So, Dale Fletcher is our man?"

Buck nodded. "They're working on tracing his phone, financials, everything."

"Is he connected to Sutton?" Evan asked as he sat down next to Bexley.

"Not sure. But if he is, I expect they'll find it."

Jeff paced the room. "Where did Haiden go?"

"One of you should've gone with him," Buck said. "We need to stay together."

"You're talking Haiden here. You wanna try and stop him?"

Buck glared at Jeff before heading for his office.

"Should we go after him?" Bexley asked.

Jeff shook his head. "I think he needs some time. He'll get here soon enough. What we need is this Dale Fletcher in custody so he can tell us who hired him to plant those fake bombs on our doorstep."

"Why would he plant fake bombs so no one would be injured but then kill the two men who helped him?" Evan leaned on the island. "It doesn't make sense."

"Nothing about any of this makes sense. Kyra and Dani getting attacked ... someone going after me too? I don't get it."

"Calm down." Bexley grabbed a bottle of water and tossed it to him. "You need to think clearly. This is your wheelhouse. What would explain these attacks separately? Then how do they connect?"

Jeff sucked down half the bottle before capping it and taking a deep breath. "Whoever attacked Kyra and Danica—that was personal. They had a plan and put it in place. I think Dani could've been in big trouble if he had gotten to her earlier. But she was too close to our office, and he backed down."

"Are we sure it's a 'he'? Some women can get pretty aggressive."

Jeff nodded at Bexley. "Yes, but I know Dani well enough to know she doesn't have very many people in her life, women included. Kyra has a small circle too—maybe three or four people she actually interacts with."

"Why?"

Jeff paced the room. "After what happened to them, Kyra

suffered from a lot of issues with PTSD. She used drugs for a while, trying to find some kind of escape. That made her an outcast to a lot of people."

"But she's clean now?"

Jeff nodded to Bexley. "According to Danica, yes. Riley didn't mention a drug angle. I'm pretty sure they would've tested her after the accident, just in case."

"So, if the attacks on them are personal, what about the other instances? You said a different-colored truck bumped Danica from behind in her hometown, then you were in the car with her and avoided a crash." Evan shrugged. "It's like two different attackers. One intense and personal, the other just wasting our time."

Jeff held out his hands. "I don't get it either."

"I'm not blaming you, man. I'm just thinking out loud."

Jeff's face heated. "I know. Sorry."

Pacing the room, Jeff twisted the bottle in his hands.

God, we need some answers here. Please. She's running out of time.

41

A groan escaped Haiden's lips as he kicked out the door of his Jeep.

He rolled into the wet mud, leaning on all fours. Based on the throbbing pain in his left shoulder, it was dislocated.

Digging through the car, he finally found his phone wedged into the dash. The screen shattered, but it still called out.

"Yeah," Jeff answered.

"Ev." He took a breath, trying to get his mind straight.

"Haiden? What's wrong?"

"I ... my Jeep, someone ..."

"Where are you?"

"I don't know." His mind shifted as he struggled to breathe. "The back road out ..."

"Buck has your signal. We're on the way."

Haiden slumped against the door, lightheaded. His mind went dark as he leaned against the Jeep.

A jolt of cold air stung at his lips, and he lifted his head. Staring down at his phone, Haiden pried his eyes open. The time read almost ten minutes after his phone call. Straining to stand, he took a deep breath as gravity pulled at every muscle.

He glanced over at the wreckage. A strange box was tucked

in the wheel well. Leaving it alone, he continued to look around the Jeep. A small wire stuck out from the steering column, singed with melted plastic around it.

Lights reflected on the Jeep as two SUVs pulled up.

"Haiden?" Bexley ran to Haiden.

He stepped back, holding his hands up.

"Bex." Evan's voice boomed in the quiet of the hillside.

She stopped short as Evan pushed past her.

Looking him over, Evan frowned. "You good?"

"Put, put my shoulder back in."

"We called an ambulance—"

Haiden pushed past Evan and Bex to Buck.

"Put it back in."

Buck shook his head. "We should wait."

"It w-wasn't ... it's not an accident."

"What?" Jeff finally arrived.

"Look for yourself. Steering locked up on me."

"How did they get to your car?" Buck pushed past him to the Jeep and assessed the wheelbase. "He's right. These are trackers, and there's a detonator of some kind on the steering column." Buck rose and peered at Haiden. "Someone had access to this car. Where've you been lately?"

Haiden leaned back against the SUV. "I ... I was at the hospital."

"Why?"

He cut his eyes to Bexley before looking back at Buck. "Then work. That's all."

"Did you go to the store? Anywhere you left the Jeep unattended?"

He shook his head.

Jeff paced, his hands fisting.

"Jeff?"

Jeff wouldn't look up at him. Haiden stood with a grunt and got in Jeff's way. "W-what is it?"

His face bright red, Jeff gripped his hips. "Tony."

Haiden's heart pounded. "H-he's got her!"

"Why Tony?"

Haiden ignored Evan, but Jeff leaned over, looking ready to lose his lunch.

"I thought you said he was a good guy, and he wanted to protect Danica?"

"It makes sense," Buck muttered. "He was at the office the other day. He works at the hospital—"

"At the hospital, he stopped and t-talked to me. Said he recognized my Jeep out front." Haiden paused. "I-I told Dani he was d-dangerous."

"What?" Jeff came out of his stupor. "Why did you think that?"

"I met him. I could tell ... this wasn't Roltz."

Evan gripped Haiden's arm, and he turned, fisting his hand as Evan backed up.

"Take it easy. Until we know for certain—"

"It's him. It's th-the only thing that makes sense," Haiden sneered, grabbing his arm and taking the weight from the joint.

"I'll do it." Bexley's voice rang out, and he turned. "I'll put your shoulder back in."

"Bex." Evan's stern voice sounded.

Haiden shook his head. "You're not strong enough."

"What?" Bexley planted her hands on her hips.

Haiden turned his gaze to Evan.

"He's right. If you've never done it before, you've got to get it right the first time." Evan shook his head and moved in front of Haiden. "You ready?"

Haiden nodded and planted his legs, gripping a tree next to him with his right arm. The sudden tug and slam took the air from his lungs for a second. He gasped in another deep breath.

"Good?"

"Better." Haiden rotated his shoulder, releasing a loud pop, then he rotated his neck.

"You're still bleeding. We need to get you stitched up." Bexley walked up, but Haiden shook his head.

"No."

Buck's face reddened. "Let's, let's get back to the office and regroup. Maybe by then, Jeff will get a hold of Tony and either rule him out or make him a suspect. I'll call the locals. Evan, you wait here."

Haiden nodded and followed the others into the SUV.

DANICA STARED AT TONY. "What have you done?" she asked between sobs.

Haiden was right. Tony had more than a storm going on—he was insane.

Tony's jaw clenched, his eyes focused on the road.

"Did you ... the fire? Have you been following me too?" Her breath hitched. "Tell me you didn't run Kyra off the road," she whispered.

"That's on you. In fact, all of this is your fault."

"You're insane." She yelped as he gripped her arm above her elbow, squeezing it so tightly she thought it would break.

"I'm not insane. I'm just taking what's mine," he growled.

"Yours? I ... I don't understand."

"Humph." He let go and re-focused on the road.

Her mind spun as their past came full force to the forefront of her thoughts. The house, the shoes, the grave.

"You owe me. Everyone else would agree," Tony snarled.

Swallowing the bile burning her throat, she nodded. "Who is Sergeant Sutton?"

"My cousin."

"You mean, he's ..." She couldn't even get out the words.

"You put his father in prison. He was glad to help. After all, it's not just my life you ruined."

"But he killed your mom," she sobbed. "He was going to kill

me too! Why ... why do you hate me?"

"How would you like it if I aired all your dirty family business on the news for the world to see? It's not like your family is perfect, Dani. Your father died because he was a drunk, and your mom basically ignored you and then forgot you even exist? Your sister went to jail and rehab for her drug use you refused to take the blame for."

His words flew like daggers into her heart. It was all true.

"Oscar was all too willing to help me out. We just needed to make sure the police department didn't interfere."

"How could you do that?"

Tony shrugged. "It wasn't us. We had this all planned out. Then Oscar got orders to stand down. It was easy for him to grab you." Tony let out a laugh. "You should've seen Haiden's face when he came charging out of that building with Buck and Jeff on his heels. They were all terrified."

"What're you going to do?" she whispered, her heart pounding in her ears. "Kill me like your uncle killed your mom?"

Her head flew forward as the car lurched to a stop. His hand went around her throat as he pulled her in close. "You're lucky I'm not him," he hissed. "My life is a disaster. Once people find out who I am, they run away, scared I'll hurt them. But he was my uncle, not my father. They don't get there's nothing of him in me."

She gasped for breath. "I can't ... can't breathe."

He released his grip. "I haven't decided what to do with you yet. Part of me wants to punish you for what you did to my life." He ran his fingers down her cheek. "But the other part wants to know just how far you'll go to make me happy."

Refusing to look him in the eye, she fell forward in the seat, tears streaming down her face.

The car jolted back to life.

God, please protect Haiden and get him out safely. I don't even care if I come out alive, but please protect Haiden. He doesn't deserve this. Please send someone to find him!

42

At the office, Haiden walked in and found Bexley with a first aid kit.

"No."

"You're bleeding."

He shook his head and went to his room. Haiden ripped off the already torn shirt and grabbed a change of clothes. He jumped in the shower to wash off the blood and dirt, then got dressed.

"God, please, help us find her. I ... I just want to be with her. I want one good thing in this life, God. Please." He took a few breaths, wiping the tears from his face as he leaned over the bed.

Finally finding some composure, he headed to the living room.

"Here's an extra phone." Evan tossed it to Haiden. "It's charged and ready to go."

"Tony's phone just rolls over to voicemail," Buck said.

Haiden turned to Buck. "His house."

Buck nodded, and the two took off toward the garage. Climbing into Buck's truck, they headed toward Tony's house.

"What happened?"

"W-when?" Haiden asked.

"Why are you bailing on her all the time?"

Haiden's jaw clenched at Buck's glare. The familiar stare of his commanding officers flashed through his mind.

"My ... dad."

"I've seen the reports, son."

"Not half of it," he muttered.

As a kid, going to the ER wasn't common. It meant police, which meant Dad would be in an even worse mood the next day when he would be released.

"But what does that have to do with you and Dani?"

"I can't know. W-what ... I can't become him."

"You won't."

He glared at Buck's frown. "Everyone keeps saying that. But they don't know. My ... dad didn't even know it w-would happen."

"You talked to your dad?"

He nodded.

"Then you know, it wasn't him. He let it happen because he didn't have God there to turn to."

"How did you know?"

Buck hesitated before speaking. "I had a talk with your dad. When he came to visit you in the hospital." Buck glanced at him. "We talked a long time. I'm just glad you're talking to him now."

"I can't be the best for her. I-I can't even talk." He fisted his hands in anger, unable to get out what he wanted to say.

"No one cares about that. The thing is, do you want to be the best for her?"

"I don't deserve her." It was the truth, plain and simple.

"Maybe not. I'm impartial, though." Buck narrowed his eyes. "Look, being deserving isn't always the answer. We aren't deserving, are we? Yet God sent his Son to die for us. He loved us that much. So, do you love her?"

"Yes." It was there now, more so than he imagined it would be.

"Then you need to do the right thing. Because I think she cares a lot about you."

He swallowed as they came up to Tony's darkened house. "He's not here."

"Good. Then we can look around."

Mail piled up on the stoop, falling from the overflowing mailbox on the porch.

"He's been gone a while."

"But we just ran into him the other day. He was at the hospital," Haiden said.

Buck shook the doorknob, but it didn't budge. Kicking at the mail on the ground, Haiden discovered a small black stone.

"Can't be," he whispered.

Leaning down with a groan, he pulled up the fake rock and opened the slot to reveal a key.

"I guess we get to see what's inside."

Haiden followed Buck into the dark house, gun drawn and at his side.

"You go through the living room. I'll take the bedrooms."

He nodded at Buck's command.

The house reeked of moldy food and an acid like smell that stung his nose and made his eyes water.

"Call Jeff."

At the sound of Buck's voice, he rushed to the bedroom as he pulled out the extra phone. Punching in Jeff's number as he turned the corner, his mouth fell open.

"Hello? Haiden?"

"Get here, now." He hung up, swallowing the bile burning his throat.

Pictures of Danica lined the walls of the large walk-in closet. Some had black *X*-marks over her face, her eyes cut out on a few others. Kyra's grin showed on one with a red circle and slash through it.

"I ... I gotta go," Haiden said through gritted teeth.

Sprinting through the front door, he tried to breathe, to

make his body take a breath. The sight of those pictures ... did he draw that circle before or after he tried to kill Kyra?

The phone buzzed, and he made himself answer.

"Yeah?"

"Do I need to call the police?" Evan's hushed voice sounded over the SUV's engine.

"Yes."

"We're on our way with Jeff. Police will follow."

Haiden hung up and leaned over, trying to contain the anger and fear gripping his body.

"Lord, please, please protect her."

HAIDEN PACED THE YARD, not able to step foot back in that house.

Jeff came to the door white as a sheet. "Oh, man," his throaty voice rose through the police chatter. "He's ... he's not going to ..."

"Easy. We'll find her." Evan led Jeff to the yard, leveling a gaze on Haiden. "You need a doctor?"

Haiden shook his head.

Jeff put his phone to his ear.

"I need to know where Tony is, right now! ... You don't understand. He's done something, and I've got to talk to him."

"The police have started the investigation. So far, no one knows where Tony is."

Haiden nodded as Evan spoke. "They ... h-have they traced his phone?" He glanced up.

Evan shrugged.

"All I know is, they can't find him. They have to get a court order to get that information."

Jeff' fisted one hand as he stared at the phone in his other hand.

"W-who was that?" Haiden cleared his throat, working his

hands and trying to keep the burgeoning pain of his injuries from taking over his senses.

"His cousin, who's a few years older than us. I ... I know they used to go on vacations somewhere. It was the same place every year, but I can't think of where they used to go. In the woods, a cabin, off grid. It would be where he would go ..."

"Jeff."

"No." Jeff glared up at Haiden. "This is all my fault. I've known Tony all my life, and I've never ever suspected him of anything like this. I'm a profiler. I should've seen it."

Haiden swallowed hard, planting his feet firmly. "How ... how could you know?"

"It's my job to know!" Jeff stepped toward him.

Haiden waited for the hit, the punch that usually followed an outburst. He could take it. Hands gripping his hips, he stood rigid, taking slow breaths.

"What're you doing?"

"You need to h-hit something. Go ahead. I ... I need you to get it out of your system, so you'll think clearer." He stood and waited, but Jeff just furrowed his eyebrows.

"You're not a punching bag, Haiden."

"I know that. But you need to get a grip. I ... I can't think like this. I need someone w-who can."

Jeff paused in front of him, shaking his head. He rubbed the back of his neck and peered at Haiden. "I didn't know you had a stutter. I thought you were just that worked up back there." Jeff shifted, his body shaking.

"It's w-why I don't talk much."

"And here we all thought you were just the strong, silent type." Jeff smirked as he nodded over his head.

Bex and Evan walked up.

"I think they got whatever warrant they were waiting for. Buck mentioned Tony's phone and looking into his financials, seeing if he's used his cards recently."

Jeff let out a breath. "He needs a secluded place to keep her.

She's smart. She'll know what to do to keep herself alive and maybe even calm him down enough to find a way out." Jeff rubbed the back of her neck. "Is Buck keeping us in the loop?"

"So far, yes, but we need someone else besides him in there. He's not doing good." Evan shook his head.

"We need help. Right now." Jeff wiped his face.

Evan put a hand on Haiden and Jeff's shoulders, and Bexley stepped into the circle. "Lord, we're coming to you empty and tired. We need answers, guidance, and protection for Danica. Give her strength and a sound mind, and show us where to go to find her. Amen."

43

"Looks like he got gas about four hours ago. A station right next to his house."

Jeff listened to the police chatter in the station. He had made Buck go back to the office to get some rest. It was taking a toll on all of them, but right now, the burden fell directly on Jeff's shoulders.

He paused at DeSalis's desk. "Anything on Dale Fletcher?"

"Nothing. No use of credit cards or bank account. His phone is still off, and we have it in the system, so the second he uses it, we'll know."

His phone vibrated in his pocket. "Powers."

"Jeff?"

"Kyra? Are you okay?"

"I'm fine, but what's going on? One of the officers came by and said they were praying for Dani. What's happened?"

Jeff clenched his teeth. "Kyra—"

"Don't placate me, Jeffrey Powers."

"I wasn't going to," he explained. "Look, I'm not exactly sure what's going on, but Tony seems to have had a breakdown, and we think he took Dani."

"Took? As in kidnapped?"

"Kyra, breathe. Take a breath." Jeff paced harder, trying to keep himself upright. "Kyra?"

"Yeah, I'm here. I just ... Tony? I don't understand."

He paused. "What don't you understand?"

"He called when I was leaving Mom's."

"Danica mentioned that. What did he say?"

"Well, I didn't tell her because I thought it was a surprise. He actually called because he wanted to know where she was. He wanted to surprise her."

"Surprise her?" His jaw jumped. "With what?"

"I don't remember." Kyra sniffed.

Taking a deep breath, Jeff closed his eyes. "Kyra, just walk me through the conversation. Slowly."

He heard her forcing deep breaths in and out in a relaxation technique.

"When I answered, he asked how things were going. I mentioned the coffee shop and my interview. He said he thought it was a great job for me. He said I'm really friendly, and it would be a good fit. Then he asked how Dani was doing. I said fine, working all the time as usual. I ... I mentioned wishing she would come home more."

"She works a lot," Jeff offered.

"Yeah, I miss her sometimes." She let out a heavy sigh. "He said she works too much, and he wanted to surprise her. He thought he could convince her to go ... go somewhere? I can't remember what he said."

Jeff's heart pounded as he sat down, snapping his fingers at DeSalis and motioning him over. He put the phone on speaker.

"Kyra, you're doing great. Just close your eyes and remember driving to the coffee shop. Did you take Main Street?"

"No, all the lights. It takes forever to get to the other side. I was driving on Wallace when he called, and then I turned on Sycamore."

"So, you're talking to Tony on Sycamore and he mentions how great it would be to give Danica a vacation, right?"

"Yeah, except he didn't say vacation. He just said a break, like he was going to go pick her up for the day. A day trip! That's what he said."

He let out a breath. "Perfect. Now, where did he say he wanted to take her? We all know she's not a traveler, so it would have to be close."

"Close by, somewhere she could unplug," Kyra muttered.

"That sounds great. Maybe the woods?"

"No, I think he mentioned a lake? Or river? I'm sorry, I just can't remember."

He took the phone off speaker and held it to his ear. "You did great. I think that will help."

"You think ... do you think he's going to hurt her?"

He swallowed the lump in his throat. "Kyra, I don't know what he's going to do. I have no idea. But I'm going to find her. Buck and me and the team. We're going to find her." His heart clenched at the sound of her sobbing. "I'll call as soon as I have something. Whose phone is this, by the way?"

"It's Tommy's, the officer here. He said I could borrow it."

Jeff nearly dropped the phone. "Great. I'll call you later." He hung up. "The phone. It's the phone!" He called Buck.

"Jeff? You found something?"

"The phone. Find Dani's phone. I was working on it in your office."

"Hang on."

"You want to explain?" DeSalis stood in front of Jeff, a frown on his face.

"Danica was trying to get her phone to work the other night when someone was chasing her down and rear-ended her car. She said it wouldn't call out. Someone had uploaded something onto the system."

"I've got it," Buck said. "What do I do with it?"

"Stay there. I have an idea." Jeff hung up and headed for the doors.

"I'm coming. I want to know what's going on."

Jeff didn't argue as he jumped into the SUV and cranked the engine.

44

Danica's legs ached as she sprinted through the brush, quietly listening for him to follow. Her ankle was now swollen, so sore she could barely run. But she wasn't going to waste this chance on getting away.

The wet leaves hit her face, and the saplings pulled at her legs, as if trying to slow her escape. Pausing behind a tree trunk, she steadied her breath and listened. So far, she hadn't heard him approach, but that wouldn't last long.

Moving once again, her body trembled, but she couldn't tell if it was fear or the fact she was soaked. An early morning shower began as soon as she escaped out the door.

She had recognized the cabin from the pictures Tony showed them from their family trips. Hopefully, Jeff would remember it as well.

The sound of a snapping branch made her pause.

Was that him?

She waited a second longer, but the sound vanished. Continuing her path, she prayed this was the way toward another cabin or a road.

The sun was just rising, and she hated it. She needed the darkness to hide her escape, to keep her hidden from Tony.

A heavy force slammed into her from behind, and she tumbled forward, bracing herself from the fall with her arms stretched out.

"You know you can't outrun or hide from me." Tony's salty breath stung her face as he pulled her up and replaced the zip ties she had worked so hard to break. Then he heaved her over his shoulder. "Now, if you don't sit still, I'm going to have to tie you down to the bed instead of the chair."

She stilled. The bed was the last place she wanted to be.

JEFF SNATCHED Danica's phone from Buck's hands.

"I thought you said that proved someone was monitoring Danica? How are you going to find who put it on there?"

Putting in the diversion code, a phone number popped up. He handed it to DeSalis. "Track this number. See if it will lead us to Tony's location. I don't recognize it, so hopefully it's not his usual phone."

"You had that the whole time?"

He glared at Buck. "I already checked it, but I couldn't find the number. Things got a little crazy before I had a chance to get it to Sutton. Good thing I didn't. He would've erased it, deleted it, or sent us after someone else."

"My guy is ready. I just need a location."

Jeff nodded at Sergio. Once Sergio had been informed about what was going on, he wasted no time calling in a few favors and showing up to help.

"It has to be that cabin," Jeff mumbled as he paced. "Tony always talked about it, and that's where his mom took them on vacation before she died."

"You mean was murdered," Bexley corrected.

"Yeah. It's also where his sister tried to commit suicide."

"Tried?"

Jeff frowned at Haiden. "She didn't mention that part?"

Haiden shook his head. Dark circles under his eyes and blood pooling under his shirt, the man appeared dead on his feet.

"After everything came out, Tony and his sister were attacked by reporters and anyone who wanted a story. It was a big deal. Something like that happening in our small town. His sister, Paulie, couldn't deal. She went to the cabin alone, and Tony called me, frantic to find her. By the time we got there ..." He shook his head at the memory. "There was a lot of blood, and she was unconscious. But we got her to the hospital in time."

"And Dani blamed herself," Haiden added.

Jeff nodded. "If Dani hadn't found Tony's mom, it would have just been a missing persons case. Even if they found the body, there's no way to know if they could've ever linked it to Tony's uncle. Danica has always blamed herself for the entire thing."

"Even though she helped to uncover a murder and a murderer?" Bexley paced back and forth. "I mean, she probably saved Tony and his sister."

"It was much closer than that," Buck said.

"Right," Jeff agreed.

It took years before Buck finally let him in on the scene when he arrived at Eugene's makeshift graveyard. Danica was wrapped in a blanket, blood seeping through and pale. Buck subdued Eugene, but wasn't able to get to Dani. She didn't respond to his calls, and Buck commented that he assumed she was already dead.

"I've got a location." DeSalis handed Sergio a piece of paper.

They all gathered around Sergio as he typed in the coordinates.

"Okay, it's coming through. My buddy says he's got a satellite that goes over that area every so many hours on its way to the coast. We just have to find the right cabin ..."

Jeff leaned in at the imaging, seeing several cabin rooftops. A white chimney popped, and he pointed. "It's that one. I remember the pictures. It has a white chimney and a white door on the front."

"Let's hope it gives us something." Sergio typed away, rewinding the footage from the last few hours.

DeSalis typed on his phone. "My guys are ready to go. We just need confirmation—"

"Oh, man," Sergio muttered.

They all peered at the computer screen and saw what appeared to be a small image running through the trees. Another image came around in front, and the smaller image collapsed.

Haiden's fist went through the wall.

"Let's get going." Buck motioned to the hallway.

Haiden stood, staring at the wall, his body shaking.

"Haiden. Now." Buck's voice dropped a register, and the sternness came out of nowhere.

Haiden's head jerked up, and he made his way to his locker, gathering his equipment as sweat dripped down his face.

Jeff pulled Buck toward the door. "You do realize he's about to drop, right?"

"He'll be fine. Best training around."

"I heard that." Evan voiced from behind them.

Buck nodded with a smirk as they all headed to the garage, Haiden bringing up the rear.

45

D anica took the water he offered, but wouldn't eat the food. As much as she wanted her strength to get away again, she needed to see just how vested Tony was in this, how far he'd go to keep her alive.

After her escape failed, he had her bound tightly to the chair, her movements basically reduced to zero.

"You need to eat."

"I'm not hungry."

Tony slammed the water bottle down on the table and stood. "After taking off like that, you think I'm going to put up with attitude too?"

Talking. She needed him talking. More time for Jeff to find her. They had to have located Haiden by now. He was probably in the hospital. Or ... She closed her eyes for a second.

God, please let him be okay.

"You know, this is where we found her."

Danica refused to look down at the floor he was pointing to.

"I bleached it, scrubbed it, but the blood won't come off."

"I'm sorry."

He scoffed. "You've said that so many times, over and over, as if that makes it all better."

"It's not to make it better."

"That's right. It's for you, isn't it? To make *you* feel better."

She shook her head.

Tony stood there, glowering over her. "When we came inside, there was blood everywhere. Her clothes were saturated, and she was so pale ..." His eyes met hers. "She left a note."

"I ... I didn't know that," she whispered.

"It said she wanted to die on her own. She wanted to take her life so no one else would take it." Tony wiped the tears from his cheeks. "Having someone close to you kill your mother, someone who was supposed to protect you and take care of you ... it makes trust hard."

He leaned into her space. "That's why she did it. If we had never known what happened, there never would've been a reason for her to be scared."

"You think not knowing is better?"

"Everyone knows how your dad died. He was drunk and ran off the road."

"I see people every day in situations where they have no idea what's happened or why. They don't know the person who tried to kill them, or who maybe killed someone they love. It doesn't make it any easier."

"Don't!" He slammed his fist on the table. "Don't try to reason this out with me. My life was taken from me the moment you went over the fence. Why did you do that? Why did you go?"

Tears streamed down her cheeks. "I just ...I don't know. I wanted to get out of the house. Mom was upset and forgetting everything and yelling at Buck all the time. Jeff didn't even come over anymore. I just wanted out." She looked up at his red face. "No one was supposed to be there."

He shook his head and paced the room for a moment in silence. "We've got to move in an hour. You've got that long to either fall asleep, or I'll put you to sleep."

"But—"

"No." He glared down at her.

She took several deep, slow breaths, working to calm her heart and her body.

Where was he going to take her? And once they got there, would he let her live?

"HAIDEN?"

Buck's voice echoed in Jeff's earpiece as he waited for Haiden's reply.

"She's ... she's there. Bound, to a chair." Haiden's deep, raspy voice finally answered.

"Okay, confirmed sighting. On my mark."

Jeff headed to the far side of the cabin. "Haiden, where's the mark?"

"Far corner by the window. Those on the north side—he'll see you." Haiden's voice was clear and perfect. Apparently, his emotions were back under wraps. "Enter the front door, push him back away from her."

Evan would go in first, followed by Sergio, then Buck. Buck's target was Danica. The other two would take care of the mark, and he would cover the back door. DeSalis was behind him with his officers, waiting for them to breech.

Buck's whispered count came through the com as he held his ground outside the back door of the cabin.

Please God, don't let us be too late.

46

D anica stiffened at the sounds of broken wood and shouts. Hands searched her body and freed her arms and legs. The familiar scent of Old Spice made her reach up. She found Buck's neck and held on. Burying her face in his shoulder as he carried her, the voices of her team echoed behind her in the cabin.

As the cold air hit her wet clothes, she shivered and pulled at his neck. "Buck, you have to—"

"Are you okay?" Buck put her gently on the ground. He held her up on her side as she kept her weight off her injured ankle.

"I'm fine, but Haiden—he blew up Haiden's Jeep. You have to find him." She gripped the front of his shirt, but Buck just kept looking her over, checking her face and her wrists. "Buck, please." Tears stung her eyes. "Stop worrying about me! You have to get Haiden!"

Buck nodded as his gaze landed over her head. She shifted and turned. Haiden stood several feet away, and her breath stalled in her lungs. The Ranger she knew, had seen in different missions over the past year, stood staring at her. That familiar connection between them heated.

He ran to her, pulling off the shoulder strap of his rifle and his ghillie suit. Then, handing the rifle to Buck, picked her up.

"Haiden, I saw the Jeep. He made me watch." Tears blinded her vision as she gripped his neck.

"You need a hospital." His voice was ragged as he carried her to the ambulance that waited down the long driveway.

"Haiden? Haiden, you're bleeding. Your neck ..." She pulled up in his arms to try and see his back when a groan came through his lips. "Put me down. You're hurt. I can walk."

"No, you can't." He sat her on the gurney and followed her into the back as an EMT started an IV.

"Haiden ..." she tried to sit up, but the EMT pushed her down and shut the doors.

Gripping his hand tightly, she waited for the medic to move to the front so she could sit up.

"Lie down."

She could see the tears forming in his eyes. Wrapping her free arm around his neck, she held him tightly. "I thought I lost you."

Leaning over, Haiden placed a soft kiss on her lips, his bright eyes staring into hers. "I thought ... I lost you."

His arms wrapped around her body, and she fell into him, her emotions finally breaking loose as she sobbed, the repercussions her nightmare finally coming to an end.

HAIDEN STAYED with the gurney as long as he could, but they wouldn't let him go into the exam room with her. He stood still, stiffly, watching the doors as he sensed Buck come up behind him.

"She okay?"

"She passed out in the ambulance, exhaustion and mild hypothermia. They're X-raying her ankle."

"Uh, Haiden? The doctor wants to look at you."

He ignored Jeff's comments as he stared at the doors.

"Haiden?"

"No."

After thirty minutes, a woman came out with a stethoscope around her neck and a name badge on her scrubs.

"She's fine. Her ankle is severely swollen but not broken. She needs to be warmed up, and she'll be here for a while on IV antibiotics for the wounds to her wrists and ankles."

Haiden nodded.

"Can we go in?"

Ignoring Buck's question, Haiden pushed past the doctor into the room.

Standing next to her bed, his heart pounded. She was pale, her hair soaking wet, and covered by a large warming blanket.

"Sit down before you pass out, son." Buck's voice came through as he took the chair next to the bed, then found her hand under the blankets.

"Sir, you're bleeding."

"He knows." Buck's stern voice echoed in the room.

"His shoulder—"

"It's not dislocated anymore."

He barely registered Evan's voice as he focused on Danica, waiting for her to wake up.

"Haiden?" Buck's stern voice broke his focus.

"Yeah." He kept his gaze on her.

"Take your shirt off. They want to stitch you up before you bleed everywhere."

He slowly stood and pulled off the tactical vest with a groan. "Cut the shirt," he muttered.

"What?"

"His shoulder, just cut it." Evan sounded exasperated.

Haiden turned the chair and sat backward so the doctor had access while he pushed back under the blankets for Danica's hand. Her lip twitched, and he felt a surge inside him. He'd wasted so much time waiting, thinking it wouldn't work, that she wouldn't accept him, or that he'd mess it all up later in life.

But he'd failed before they even started.

"Get dressed."

He looked up at Buck, who held a change of clothes. He started to speak, but Buck held his hand up.

"Bathroom is there. Go and change."

He nodded and stood slowly, his back seizing up. The long hours without sleep and the let-down of adrenaline made a move on his body.

In the bathroom, he removed his boots and cargo pants and changed. Washing his face in the sink, he let out a breath as the cool water eased his muscles. He dried off and pulled on the shirt with a grunt, the sting of whatever the doctor had done to his back burning to his core.

As he stepped out, Buck sat on the chair next to Danica, his hand pushing the hair from her face. Buck was like her father, but Haiden had stepped in and taken care of her without thought. As hard as it was on him, he knew Buck had to be taking it harder. He waited by the foot of the bed, gripping the rail and waiting for her to wake up.

Evan brought a chair over for him and pushed him into it as Bexley put a cup of coffee in his hand. These people, the ones he hid from for so long, were his family. God had given him something good in this life—these people who surrounded him.

Evan had a hold on Bexley, and Jeff and Sergio leaned against the wall. Jeff was a wreck. His face showed the strain of feeling like he'd failed. But the truth was, if it hadn't been for him, they wouldn't have found out so much about Tony.

"Danica?"

Haiden stood when Buck spoke, and her eyes fluttered open.

"Oh, I ..." She started to sit up, but Buck gently put her back down. "What ... where am I?"

"In the hospital. You're safe. Tony's in custody."

Her eyes blinked several times, then locked onto his.

"We just wanted to stay until we knew you were okay." Jeff walked up and tugged on her hand. "You gave us a scare."

"You have no idea," she whispered through trembling lips.

"Let's go." Evan's voice pulled everyone from the room, except Haiden and Buck.

Buck stood and kissed Danica on the head. "Don't scare me like that again, Dani girl."

"Yes, sir," her voice barely above a whisper.

Buck turned and faced Haiden. "Remember what we talked about." He slapped him on his good arm and walked away.

"What ... what did you talk about?" She hid her face partially under the blankets.

He pulled the chair up to the bed and found her hands. "Just stuff." He smirked as he pulled down the blanket from her face.

Her eyes watered, and she tried to hold back, but it did no good. Sitting on her bed, he pulled her into his lap, wrapping the blankets around her. She cried, her arms gripping his neck.

He kissed her head. "I'm sorry, Danica."

"What? This is all my fault." She took a deep breath. "He was after me and went after you because—"

"Don't." He eased her back, pulling the hair from her face, and then wiped her tears away. "This is not your fault."

"Then how can you say it's yours?"

He sighed and pulled her in close again, hugging her and feeling peace now that she was safe. "I'm sorry about ... everything. Everything I've done to you to hurt you. I let my pride get in my w-way. You deserve better."

"What does that mean?"

His whole body shivered, and he whispered into her ear. "It means, I don't know w-what to do without you, Dani. In all my life, I've not asked for anything. Until you. I just w-want you."

She leaned back. Her eyes glistened as she stared up at him. "I didn't think you could?"

"I've got a lot to talk to you about before you actually agree."

She managed a smile and leaned back into his neck. As much as he wanted to hold her, she needed rest.

"You should lie down."

"Are you leaving?"

"Not a chance." He sighed and leaned into the side of her face, kissing her cheek. Easing her back to the bed, he wrapped her up and sat next to her, holding her hand.

"What is it?" she whispered. Her eyes fluttered in an attempt to stay awake.

"Get some rest. I'll be here when you wake up."

"Promise?"

He gave her a gentle kiss, and her eyes popped open. "I told you, I'm not going anywhere."

She nodded and closed her eyes, her jaw relaxing as she drifted to sleep.

47

J eff watched as Tony lay in the hospital bed.

After breeching the cabin, shots sounded while Buck removed Danica from harm's way. Inside, Tony lay on the ground, gripping his arm and Evan standing over him. Tony had gone for the gun sitting on the table.

It was likely the same gun he'd used to kill Oscar Burnett, Oscar Sutton.

"You talk to him?"

Jeff shook his head at Buck's question.

"You should."

"He killed his cousin, kidnapped and hurt Danica, and I never saw it. How did Haiden see it?"

Buck sighed. "When you see evil every day, you recognize it."

His eyes cut to Buck. "He warned Dani."

Buck nodded. "I don't think she was convinced, either."

"I just ... after everything we've been through, how did I not see this?"

"You can't do that." Buck set his hand on Jeff's shoulder. "This isn't on you. Danica doesn't blame you, and neither do I."

Jeff did his best to swallow the lump in his throat. "I was there when we found Paulie. Tony called in, hysterical, saying she left a note. We went to the cabin. There was blood everywhere. I didn't think she'd make the drive out.

"We stood like this, outside the room, and waited in silence for her to wake up. I don't even remember how long we waited before Tony said, 'I can't live like this.' I asked what that meant, and he said he couldn't lose Paulie. She was the last real family left in his life."

Buck let out a sigh. "She passed away a few weeks ago."

"What?" Jeff turned, his jaw agape, as he stared at Buck.

"Riley called earlier, told me he found out when he started looking through the footage of the truck. It was hers, registered in her name. When she passed, Tony made a scene. The security at the McMasters Institute handled it, and they didn't call the police. He never had a funeral, never accepted anything about her death. The coroner called the facility and learned she was to be cremated, so they took care of it."

"It was her death," Jeff whispered as he leaned back against the wall. "That's what triggered all this. He lost her and still blamed Danica."

"It doesn't explain everything."

Jeff frowned. "What?"

"Sutton didn't have a red pickup truck. Neither does Tony. I had DeSalis check everyone in their circle to see what they drove, and there's not one there."

"What about the men? Any connection to Sutton? Did they find Dale Fletcher?"

"DeSalis is checking that angle, and no, still nothing on Fletcher."

Jeff shook his head. "Fletcher is probably a dead end by now. Literally."

"I agree."

Staring through the blinds at a resting Tony, Jeff's jaw tensed. If Tony wasn't running the whole thing, then who was responsible?

DANICA WOKE UP WITH A START. The sound of footsteps in the brush roused her. Sitting up, her body seized as the muscles strained and voiced their disapproval of being pulled even more.

Taking a few breaths, she opened her eyes and found herself in a hospital room. She was safe, no longer in the woods. Rolling on her side, Haiden sat, passed out in the fold-out recliner, his face resting and sporting more than just a shadow.

"Lord, thank you," she whispered softly, her heart bursting at the man who God had saved for her.

He saved Haiden in so many ways. Getting him out of the house with his father and saving his soul, saving him from the service he was in for his country and helping him get out alive. Saving him from the Jeep crash that still haunted her memories.

God had rescued him, and he had a purpose in this life. She could only pray that it would be to save her as well. Save her from her loneliness, her pride, her selfishness. He was the exact opposite of those things and would give up everything for anyone who needed something.

She studied his face with a smile. Haiden had her attention the second they met. He was muscular with a strong, square jaw, beautiful green eyes that brightly shone under mile long eyelashes.

Leaning back in bed, she watched him sleep, wishing he would curl up with her instead, keep her warm and hold her. Her body shivered, even with all the blankets.

He suddenly bolted upright and scanned the room, finding her quickly. A smile spread across her face.

Oh man, that smile.

"Did you sleep?"

"A little."

He sat on the bed, felt her forehead, and frowned.

"What?"

"You're still pretty cold."

"I know, I ... I need something besides two hospital gowns."

He pulled out his phone. "Maybe Bexley can bring you something." He handed her the phone, and she scrolled through the contact list.

"Haiden?"

"Hey."

"Hey! How are you feeling? Are you okay?"

"I'm cold. Could you bring me some sweats and socks and clean everything?" She smiled as Haiden rubbed her legs through the blankets, warming her.

"Of course. What about Haiden?"

She lowered the phone to her chin. "Bex wants to know if you need anything."

He shook his head.

"No. I guess he's fine."

"He's not, but that's okay."

"What do you mean?" She narrowed her eyes at Haiden as he paused.

"He has a dislocated shoulder and collarbone that needs to be set properly, and—"

"You have a dislocated shoulder and collarbone?"

He frowned, and as he straightened, the left side drooped.

"Food. Have them bring food."

"Bex, can you bring some food too? I've got to go." She hung up and glared at Haiden. "How on earth did you carry me with a dislocated shoulder and collarbone? And I'm sure you were set up to shoot if you had to."

"I set up on my right side."

"Haiden, please, you need a brace. They need to look at it. Who put it back?"

"Evan."

She groaned and leaned back in the bed. A shiver moved through her as he pulled her blankets up. Taking advantage of him leaning up to her, she gripped his shirt to hold him in place.

"Please get checked out. I'm assuming it's from the crash. You didn't let them look at it, did you?"

"A doc stitched up my back—"

"Your back?" She worked to ease her breathing as she let go and curled into the blankets, covering her face with her hands and holding back her tears as much as she could.

"Danica, I'm okay. Really. I ... I'll wear a brace if you w-want me to." He sat next to her and leaned over her body, rubbing her back. "Talk to me."

She took in a few breaths as sobs pushed through her chest. "Haiden, I ... I watched you go over that ravine, okay? I saw the Jeep disappear into the trees, but I was tied up, and I couldn't do anything but watch and scream and ..."

He wrapped her in a hug while she wept. Her whole body shook, weak, dazed and dizzy.

"You're too cold."

She closed her eyes and Haiden kissed her cheek.

"Please, just hold on."

With a deep breath, she faded away again.

48

"How's she holding up?" Buck entered and paused at her bedside.

"She's better. Her temp is climbing, but still not normal." Haiden rotated his shoulder with a wince.

"What set her off?"

He looked up as Buck glared down at him.

"Bexley said she was upset."

"She was, after Bexley told her I wasn't okay and had dislocated my shoulder."

"That set her off?"

Haiden leaned back and nodded to the extra chair from earlier. Buck sat down.

"Tony made her w-watch my wreck."

"Yeah. She told me," Buck's deep voice resonated as he sat up and leaned on his knees.

"She got worked up and started crying. She said they were w-watching when my Jeep went off the road and into the ravine. All she could do was scream because she was tied up."

"DeSalis needs to get in here and interview her. All this needs to get recorded for the prosecution. Between that and what we found at his house, it should be enough."

"What're you talking about?" Danica's eyes were open, watching them intently as she lay in bed.

"What did you hear?" Buck stood.

"In the house. What did you find?"

"Pictures, honey. He had taken a lot of pictures of you and a few of Kyra too." Buck's voice turned soft, almost a whisper as he spoke.

Her face paled even more, and Haiden stood, holding her hand.

"Dani, I need to know what happened. Did you see Sutton?"

She took a few breaths. "I ... we got into the car because it was cold. He sprayed something that made me cough, and then I passed out. I didn't see him after that." Her teary eyes met Haiden's. "He's really ... the man who tried ..."

"I know." He sat down next to her. "We know."

"Do you know what happened to him?"

Wiping her eyes, she turned to Buck. "No. I didn't see him when I woke up, and Tony didn't say anything ..." Her voice trailed off, and she furrowed her brows.

"What do you remember?"

"Shouting, and then ... I think gunshots? I couldn't move, and my eyes wouldn't open. What happened to him? Is he in custody?"

Haiden glanced at Buck, and Buck nodded.

"What?"

He sighed. "Tony shot him, Dani."

"Oh, my word," she whispered.

A knock sounded on the door, and Bexley walked in with Evan. "Everything okay?"

"I've been better."

"I've got clean clothes and food."

Haiden leaned in and kissed her forehead. "You still feel cool. Be careful getting up and around. Okay?"

"Yeah, thanks," she whispered.

Squeezing her hand, he stood and headed out the door. Evan and Buck followed.

Collapsing in the waiting area chairs, Haiden leaned his head back and let out a groan when his shoulder complained.

"You should take something," Buck grunted.

"Yeah, or get it checked out." Evan's voice echoed in the empty room.

"Won't do much good." Haiden swallowed and popped his neck.

"Which one? Medicine or getting checked out?" Buck grinned.

"Either. Pain meds don't work. Have to knock me out."

Evan shook his head and sat next to Haiden. "You're tougher than you look." A smile crossed Evan's face. "So, how does it feel to be vexed yourself, Haiden?"

Buck and Evan laughed as Haiden let out a smile. The term he so eloquently used to describe Bexley and Evan's whirlwind romance was now being thrown in his face. But he didn't mind. It just meant God had a plan, and he was good at waiting.

"Are you smiling?" Jeff rounded the corner, carrying a bouquet of flowers.

"He's just vexed." Evan winked at him, and Jeff chuckled.

"What goes around, comes around, Haiden."

"Hey, hang out here. She's changing."

Jeff nodded at Buck and leaned against the wall. "Did she say anything?"

"He made her watch my wreck," Haiden mumbled. Fisting his hand, all he could think of was getting her out of this hospital and away from Tony forever.

"She thought she remembered gunshots, but nothing else about Sutton once she blacked out in the cruiser."

"Fletcher?"

Haiden glanced up at Evan's question, but Jeff just shook his head. They were all thinking the same thing. Although Tony was obviously a danger, he wasn't behind the entire chaos that surrounded them.

This case was far from over.

49

"Wow."

Danica stepped into the garage and found Haiden staring—a brand new Jeep was parked in the garage behind him. After a few days in the hospital and a week of sitting around the office, she and Haiden were going on their first date. She was more than ready.

"You look amazing."

She grinned as he pulled her in for a squeeze.

"When you texted me to meet you in the garage, I had no idea you'd bought a new Jeep."

A flush came over his face as he ran his fingers through her hair. "I wanted to surprise you." He took a breath. His eyes danced as he held her hand tightly.

"A surprise, huh?"

"I wanted you to be the first to ride in it with me." He grinned his amazing smile that almost knocked her over.

"I would love to." She chuckled as he pulled her in, leaned down, and kissed her cheek.

"You're beautiful, Danica," he whispered in her ear.

Her heart pounded, and goosebumps covered her body. He chuckled, and she knew he had seen them, felt them, whatever.

No reason to pretend anyway. She was too far gone when it came to Haiden Blake.

He opened her door, and she slid in, grinning. The Jeep was beautiful. Leather interior, a cherry black color. She loved it. Haiden entered the driver's side, smiling.

"You excited?"

"Yeah. Never had a new car before."

As he backed out, she watched his face shine. He reached for her hand, and she gripped his tightly, pushing her fingers through his.

"You know, it took you long enough to ask me out for an official date."

He sighed, shaking his head. "I was worried about you. You're exhausted. I know you're not sleeping. My room is right below yours."

"Sorry."

The nightmares had been so frequent, it took a lot for her to get any rest at night.

"From now on, if you have a nightmare, I'm coming up."

"No, Haiden, you still have work. You need to sleep."

"I'm used to no sleep." He frowned and pulled her hand to him, making her shift in the seat as he kissed her fingers. "I'm sorry I waited so long. All you had to do was ask. I'll go wherever you want, babe."

"Glad to know it's that simple. I'll keep it in mind." She chuckled. "By the way, did you go see your dad?"

He nodded. "He's doing a little better. The doctor's still not sure if it will be enough to take care of all the cancer. He waited so long."

She squeezed his hand.

"But it might give us a little more time."

"Time is a good thing. Maybe I can go with you the next time you visit."

His jaw jumped.

"Whenever you're ready, Haiden. Just know I'm willing

to go."

He glanced over with a smile. "Thanks."

After a romantic dinner, Haiden escorted her back to the Jeep and grinned.

"What's that for?"

"You'll see."

He took the ramp off the highway and headed to a cul-de-sac, pulling into a small bungalow at the end.

"Where are we?"

He gave her a wink and slid down from the seat. Opening her door, he grabbed her hand and led her inside.

"Haiden?"

"I rent this place when I'm not at work. I know the owners." He grinned and pulled her through the living room and kitchen to the back door.

She smiled as she stepped onto the back deck. A fire ring was set up with chairs and a cooler.

"What do you have planned?"

"Just thought you might like a fire."

She sat at the ring, opened the cooler and found everything for s'mores inside, along with a few water bottles.

"I debated between cookie dough or s'mores ... but the s'mores go better with the fire."

"You do know me." She winked and stacked marshmallows on the sticks he had ready.

After laughing and talking and eating the sticky, melted treats, she wrapped up in the blanket he brought out and gazed at the sky. Here in the small neighborhood, they were far enough away from the city lights that the stars were visible.

"This is perfect, Haiden."

"Come here." Haiden eased her out of her chair and moved her beside him on a lounge chair, wrapping her up in his arms.

"Now it really is perfect." She rested her head against his chest, breathing him in and warming up.

"Dani, I ... I need you to know about my ..." he sighed heavily. "My past."

She sat up and looked into his eyes. "Haiden, you don't have to."

"Yes, I do. I don't w-want you to be ... I want you to know." He shifted his focus as she pulled his hand into hers and rested it on his chest. "I didn't talk, because of this. It just made him mad. I had lots of trips to the ER, lots of bad situations with some bad people."

"I'm so sorry," she whispered, tears filling her vision. "You're not him."

His green eyes gazed into hers. "I don't w-want to be. But the thing is, I'll never ... never be certain. He said it was his job that messed him up." He took a breath. "He let the world win. I have a lot of scars, Dani. I don't have anything to offer you. No family or—"

"Stop right there." She frowned and straightened up. "This isn't about me. You already have everything to offer me, so don't try to take that away by thinking you can't give me what I need. I don't care about your scars. Your past isn't your fault, and it doesn't define you."

Biting her cheek, she worked to keep her emotions down. "I don't want you to think you can't give me everything because of what happened to you. I love you, Haiden. I have for a long time."

His eyes searched hers as he held her arms. Even in his silence, she could see his surprise. He held her close as they hugged. He kissed her cheek and fingered her jaw. Tipping her chin upward, he kissed her lips gently.

"I love you, Danica."

"Haiden, don't—"

"It's always been you. From the moment I met you ... it w-was different. You didn't push, you didn't ... question me." He sighed and closed his eyes for a moment, then opened them and found hers. "I've searched you out each day because I ... I wwanted to be near you." His fingers moved across her cheeks, and his gaze followed.

Leaning in, she offered another kiss, lightly pressing against his lips, and smiled at the taste of chocolate and marshmallow.

"W-what?" He grinned as his eyes shifted back and forth between hers.

"After everything that's happened, I still can't believe we're here. God has an amazing plan," she whispered and ran her fingers across the stubble on his chin.

Haiden wasted no time and kissed her again. She pushed into him, deepening the kiss as he gripped her body and held her tightly. After a moment, he pulled away. His eyes widened.

"Sorry," he whispered.

"Why?" She chuckled and rested her head against his chest.

"I just ... that was ..."

She let out another laugh. "Yes, it was, but you don't need to apologize." She raised up and looked at him. "You can kiss me like that anytime."

"No, I don't think I can." He grinned.

She smiled and went back to his chest, snuggling into his body as he covered her up with the blanket. His strong arms held her, and she sighed.

"Something on your mind?" He kissed her head.

"I guess I never thought we would make it. There's just so much past to wade through." She smiled at his squeeze.

"I'll help you through anything. Just tell me what you need."

"You, Haiden. I just need you." She pulled up and kissed his neck, then slid back down to rest on his chest. "I love you."

"I love you too."

50

Target practice had always been the worst. She could shoot, but distance wasn't her friend. She was more of a close shot while clearing the room type shooter. Setting up in the box, Danica took a deep breath and squeezed the trigger.

"Better." Haiden's voice came over the com and she grinned.

As Haiden worked with her, she found the passion he had for the one thing he professed to be good at, and it made her smile.

"One more, Dani."

She closed her eyes for a moment, cleared her thoughts, and settled her heartbeat. As she opened them, she released the safety and focused on her aim. Breathing through, she squeezed the trigger again.

"Dead center! Great shot!"

She jumped up, seeing Haiden's grin. Man, she loved him so much.

"We'll keep that one." He winked, then climbed out of the box and turned toward her.

Taking her rifle, he pulled her in by the waist and kissed her. She held him tightly and reveled in him for a moment, forgetting the fact everyone would be standing around, watching.

"That was a great shot, Dani," he whispered, his breaths coming out just as quickly as hers.

"Thanks. That was some kiss, Haiden." She grinned as his face flushed red, the grin falling to a smirk.

"Easy."

"I was just thinking about telling you the same thing." She winked at his chuckle and headed down the range to collect her target.

After almost a month of reeling, they were finally making up for lost time. Dealing with nightmares, injuries and their new relationship around everyone—things were becoming normal again.

They walked into the office, and Bexley ran toward her.

"We're engaged!"

Danica's mouth dropped as she stared at a grinning Bexley and Evan. "What? I mean, congratulations! I'm so happy for you." She snagged a hug from both of them as tears formed in Bexley's eyes. "You okay?"

"Yeah, of course." Bexley wiped her eyes with the back of her hand. "I wasn't really expecting it."

Evan shrugged. "I thought it was a great surprise." He muffled a puff as Bexley popped his arm.

"We had decided on no presents for Valentine's Day."

"It's almost two weeks past Valentine's Day, so this isn't really for that. You want me to take it back?"

"Not a chance." Bexley narrowed her eyes. "I just hope you know what you're in for."

Evan winked. "Absolutely."

"So, when's the big day?" Jeff gave Bexley a hug.

Evan shrugged. "It's up to her."

"I'm not in a hurry. I've got time to plan. Maybe a spring wedding?"

"Not in a hurry? Spring's only a few months away." Danica grinned as Evan's face turned red. "But then again, I guess you two have been holding back for a while now."

"Speaking of holding back," Jeff smirked as he cut his eyes between her and Haiden. "I'm just wondering who else is holding back."

Danica's face heated as Jeff let out a chuckle.

———

SITTING on the couch watching a movie, Danica smiled as Haiden came up behind her.

"Hey."

"Come, sit." She grinned as he rounded the couch.

She leaned forward, and his arm immediately went around her. Resting her head on his shoulder, she breathed him in and smiled.

"About what Jeff said—"

She sat up, shaking her head. "Don't. I already had a conversation with him."

"But we haven't talked about it, Dani," he whispered as he rubbed her back, searching her eyes.

"Oh. I mean, it's kinda early to be ... I mean, there's a lot we haven't ..." she found herself at a loss for words.

He set her legs in his lap and wrapped his arms around her waist. "W-what do you want?"

"Haiden, we've only just started dating, and I ..." His green eyes dart around her face, and she continued, "Honestly, I've just wanted to be with you for so long, I haven't thought about anything else."

He kissed her gently a few times before releasing her. "I want you too. So, what does that mean?"

Nerves flooded her body. What was he asking here?

"I'm not talking right now. I'm not asking right now." He frowned. "As much as I love you, I don't think ... I know I'm not ready."

"Okay. Good to know." She swallowed. "Then I'd say I want to get married one day."

"You would still do this job?"

She nodded. "This job is important to me, just like it is to you." She bit her lip. "We never really talked about that, but we'll both be in danger when we work, and we'll just ... I mean, we'll have to deal somehow."

He nodded. "You don't want me to quit?"

She shook her head. "No, and I wouldn't ask you to."

He nodded again. His fingers moved along her back. "What else do you want?"

She shuddered a little at his touch, the questions, and his soft voice.

Man, she was in deep.

"Haiden, look at me." She made his eyes find hers. "I honestly haven't given it much thought. Maybe you should tell me what you want or don't want."

He swallowed. "I'm not sure ... I ..." He dropped his gaze, and it clicked.

"You know, if we do get to that place and get married someday, maybe even have a family one day, I know you'll be a good dad, Haiden. A great one, actually."

His eyes widened. "You ... you can't know," he whispered.

"I can. Just like with us. You've let that lie hold you back for so long, thinking you'll become him. But I know you won't. Number one, you have God to guide you, and you look to Him. Number two, I wouldn't let you get like that." She grinned as a smirk found his face.

"But I know you'll be a great dad, because you're kind, strong, and loving. You know what it takes because you didn't have it." She leaned forward and kissed him gently. "I love you, Haiden. But I'm not looking at being a mom anytime soon, okay?"

He chuckled. "What about a wife?"

She felt her face heat. "I ... I mean, yes, one day." She searched his eyes. The calm that always surrounded him surfaced, and she smiled as he grinned.

He pulled her in close, leaning his forehead to hers. "I love you, Danica. More now than I did yesterday." He sighed. "I w-want to marry you. I've waited my, my whole life for you. Just tell me when."

Her body ached as her heart tried to push her brain much farther than where they should be right now. She loved him, wanted to marry him, and wanted to be with him forever. But that forever didn't have to happen right now.

"You just said you weren't ready."

"I know. I've been fighting that point." He smiled. "Let's just ... let's not wait too long, okay?"

She smiled, the comment making her breathe deeply. "Not too long, then."

He pulled her in and kissed her deeply.

"I love you, Haiden. You've been on my mind so long, I'm just so glad I have you."

He wrapped his strong arms around her. "Love you, Dani."

EPILOGUE

P acing the room, Louis clenched his jaw.

"Another win for this team means another nail in our campaign. We can't keep pushing for police reform that could possibly dismantle a successful group like this. We should re-evaluate."

Louis shook his head at his advisor, Brandon Goss's commentary. "With that many people in a group, there has to be someone who has demons we can unearth. Find me something that can throw some bad press on them and make it stick."

"Like what?" Brandon asked. "They've saved a woman and her family from a terrorist, and now they've exposed a dirty cop, saving one of their own in the process. Posting that woman's sister and her injuries in front of social media has bolstered their position and given them an edge. We might have to find another way to campaign."

"No!" Louis glared at Brandon. "I've been paid to take care of this situation, and I'll do what I must in order to unravel this mess."

Brandon stood, a grim stare focused on Louis. "Look, I never signed up to destroy someone who's doing right. You want to win this way, you find another advisor."

"You can't just walk away now. You'll never be able to work in this city, in any city, as an advisor for any campaign."

"Are you threatening me?"

Louis huffed. "I've got backers with deep pockets who're determined to undermine what's been set up. You better be thinking more and more about self-preservation for you and your family. You leave now, your mouth better stay shut."

Brandon snagged his briefcase from the couch and marched to the door. "Don't call me anymore, and don't contact me. I'm out." He turned. "And you can tell your backers that as well. If I even think me or my family are being threatened, I'll take it to the press. Just remember, I know the majority of your backers. They keep me safe. I'll keep quiet."

Louis fisted his hands as Brandon left. If he couldn't find a way to shut down this group, his campaign would suffer.

And so would he.

ABOUT THE AUTHOR

Cindy lives with her husband Garrett in rural Arkansas. They have two children, Conner and Kenzie, and are surrounded by farmland and cattle. With a full-time job, a part-time job and being a mom, carving time for her writing has become an art!

Cindy is a past semifinalist in the American Christian Fiction Writers (ACFW) Genesis award contest with her novel, *Hostage*.

She enjoys writing strong female characters and has a heart for military stories. Her creative streak a mile wide, she dabbles in photography, scrapbooking and anything else that lets her creativity loose!

OTHER TACTICAL RESPONSE TEAM BOOKS

Fighter

Book One of the Tactical Response Team (TRT)

https://scrivenings.link/fighter

Survivor

Book Three of the Tactical Response Team (TRT)

Coming November 8, 2022, from Scrivenings Press.

scrivenings.link/tacticalresponseteam

OTHER BOOKS BY CINDY BONDS

Rainstorm

by Cindy Bonds

Laurel Ashburn has a scarred past, filled with corruption and pain. After an injury overseas sends her home, she moves back in with her foster mother and to a town that hates her. Being home puts her on a path to find a missing friend. But when she's attacked over and over, who will be willing to help?

Detective Dev Hollister traded in the big city for a slower pace and less crime in rural Arkansas. After rescuing Laurel from an attempted kidnapping, he finds himself intrigued with this headstrong and stubborn woman.

While Dev's job is to protect Laurel, he wants much more than to solve the case. He wants to give her a new life and reason to stay.

Laurel will have to push beyond her dark past to trust Dev with her life. But after losing so much, can Laurel survive one more storm?

Hostage

by Cindy Bonds

Her confidence shot, Agent Macy Packer desperately wants to go back to her regular life, before she was taken hostage. To forget the pain, the fear and forget the man that helped her through all of it, then disappeared.

Kane Bledsoe is finally healed, his scars serving as a reminder of his time in captivity. But all he can think about is the blue-eyed woman that saved him. She had saved them all and left him with a burning hope.

A chance meeting and an attack prove Macy is still in danger. Kane pushes himself into the investigation, doing what he can to provide protection.

The enemy is clear, he wants Macy.

Kane will have to decide just how far he's willing to go to protect her. Can he sacrifice himself when the time comes?

MORE ROMANTIC SUSPENSE FROM SCRIVENINGS PRESS

Sharktooth Island

Trouble in Pleasant Valley

Book Three

A fabled island that no one dares to tame.

This collection contains four novellas:

Book 1 - Out of the Storm (1830) by Susan Page Davis

Laura Bryant sails with her father and his three-man crew on his small coastal trading schooner. After a short stay in Jamaica, where she meets Alex Dryden, an officer on another ship, the Bryants set out for their home in New England.

In a storm, they are blown off course east of Savannah, Georgia, to a foreboding island. Captain Bryant tells his daughter he's heard tales of that isle. It's impossible to land on, though it looks green and inviting from a distance. It has no harbor but is surrounded by dangerous rocks and cliffs.

Pirates outrun the storm and decide to bury a cache of treasure on this island and return for it later. On board is Alex, whom the cutthroats captured in Jamaica and forced to work for them. Alex risks his own life to escape the pirates and tries to help Laura and Captain Bryant outwit them. Beneath the deadly struggle, romance blossoms for Laura.

Book 2 - *A Passage of Chance* (1893) by Linda Fulkerson

Orphaned at a young age, Melody Lampert longs to escape the loveless home of the grandmother who begrudgingly raised her. Stripped of her inheritance due to her grandmother's resentments, Melody discovers her name remains on the deed of one property—an obscure island off the Georgia coast that she shares with her cousin. But when he learns the island may contain a hidden pirate treasure, he's determined to cheat her out of her share.

Ship's mechanic Padric Murphy made a vow to his dying father—break the curse that has plagued their family for generations. To do so, he must return what was taken from Sharktooth Island decades earlier—a pair of rare gold pieces. His opportunity to right the wrong arrives when his new employer sets sail to explore the island.

After a series of unexplainable mishaps occur, endangering Padric and his boss's beautiful cousin Melody, he fears his chance of breaking the curse may be ruined. But is the island's greed thwarting his plans? Or the greed of someone else?

Book 3 - *Island Mayhem* (1937) by Elena Hill

Louise Krause stopped piloting to pursue nursing, but when money got too tight she was forced to give up her dreams and start ferrying around a playboy who managed to excel during the Great Depression. When a routine aerial tour turns south, Louise is unable to save the plane.

After crash landing, the cocky pilot is stranded. She longs to escape the uninhabited island, but her makeshift raft sinks, and she and her companions are in even worse trouble. Can Louise learn to trust the others in order to survive, or will the island's curse and potential sabotage lead to her demise?

Book 4 - *After the Storm* (*present day*) by Deborah Sprinkle

Mercedes Baxter inherited two passions from her father—a love for Sharktooth Island, a spit of land in the middle of the ocean left to her in his will, and a dedication to the study of the flora and fauna on and around its rocky landscape.

For the last five years, since graduating from college, Mercy led a peaceful, simple life on the island with only her cat, Hawkeye, for company. Through grant money she obtained from a conservancy in Savannah, she could live on her island while studying and writing about the plants and animals there. Life was perfect.

But when a hurricane hits the island, Mercy's life changes for good. Her high school sweetheart, Liam Stewart, shows up to help her with repairs, and ignites the flame that has never quite died away. And if that's not enough, while assessing the damage to the island, they make a discovery that puts both their lives in danger.

Scrivenings PRESS

Quench your thirst for story.
www.ScriveningsPress.com